Cabin Fever

Debby Mayne

.
ISBN-10:1-946939-14-5
ISBN-13:978-1-946939-14-2

Chapter 1

"Don't be so hardheaded, Autumn. You need to cancel your cruise." Mama's voice cracked over the phone.

People have called me hardheaded all my life, so it didn't faze me in the least. Plus I've been teaching seventh grade English for years, and I figured if if I could put up with their hormonal mood swings, I can deal with anything. "I've been looking forward to this cruise all year."

"But people have died on that boat."

"The reports were that they died of germs."

"Exactly. I know you're healthy, Autumn, but some germs—"

"Yes, but think of it this way. After those people died, they cleaned the ship from top to bottom. I don't think there's a single germ left on that boat." I did my best to keep her from hearing doubt in my voice. I was a tad nervous too, but I'd already spent hard-earned money on this cruise, and I couldn't afford to waste a

1

penny.

"But what if—?"

"Please, Mama, don't do this. I'm going, and that's all there is to it."

"I can't talk you out of it?"

"Afraid not." I smiled as I imagined her expression of defeat. "Trust me. I'll be just fine. I'm healthier than most people, and don't forget that a lot of people on that boat *didn't* die."

"Maybe I'll see if Summer can go with you. You can use someone to help look after you."

"I don't need a bodyguard. All I need is a week of relaxing on the open sea, some delicious meals I don't have to cook, and a little time away. It's been a rough year."

After we got off the phone, I had no doubt Mama would call Summer Walsh, my first cousin who has been trying to get away from law enforcement after leaving the Nashville Police Department. The only problem is she keeps stumbling over dead bodies everywhere she goes, which makes me wonder why Mama would want her to go on the cruise with me. That's almost like asking for trouble.

Regardless of how I tried to brush off Mama's worries, as though they didn't bug me too, I was concerned enough to have nightmares. The exact boat I booked a month after school started was the one where a couple of people died from unknown causes. News sources stated that they'd contracted some sort of super bug, so the cruise company docked the ship and gave it a major scrub-down with the strongest disinfectant known to man. They even sent out a letter to everyone who'd booked a cruise and assured us that we were getting the cleanest boat in the fleet. But still …

~

After another week and at least a half dozen more phone lectures from Mama, I stood at the port in Miami, waiting to board the ship. I looked around at all the other people who'd arrived early—more couples than singles—buzzing past me, most of them excited about what we were about to experience. Naturally, there were a few bored looking people who had clearly done this enough times to lose their fascination with cruising, but I suspected that was a façade.

One of the things that always bugged my friends was my propensity to be early … for everything. Whether it was the first day of class or a party, if I arrived when I was supposed to, in my mind, I was late.

I kept glancing at my watch, until the time finally came to head to the terminal, where I was told to check in. My luggage was supposed to be waiting for me in my room … er, cabin, and I said a silent prayer that it would be there. I'd checked it when I first arrived, and it just sat there, unattended, making me wish I'd waited just a little bit longer to let it go.

After standing in the same spot for almost half an hour, I realized the line wasn't budging. I turned around and made eye contact with the person behind me who was an older man wearing a Hawaiian shirt and plaid shorts. It took every ounce of self-restraint to keep from laughing as I thought he'd gotten his fashion cues from watching too many episodes of "The Love Boat."

The line started to move a few minutes later, and I finally got to the person who asked for all of my documents. Since this was going out over international waters, I had to have a passport. The woman studied it, looked at my face, and then went back to perusing my passport again. I wasn't sure what she was thinking, but her actions made me squirm.

I had to fill out a questionnaire regarding sickness. That was fine, but I couldn't help but wonder how many people were honest. If they'd paid what I did for the cruise, they weren't likely to divulge the toilet-hugging stomach bug they had yesterday. Then she told me to stand behind the blue line so she could snap a picture of me. The image was about as flattering as my driver's license photo.

Finally, she gave me a hint of a smile and nodded, letting me know I could board. Some of my friends had warned me to bring a light carryon—one that was big enough for essentials in case my luggage got lost but not too big, or I'd be tied up with someone rummaging through my stuff. They were right. I got right through, while other passengers stood around with scowls on their faces.

On the way to the ship that was big enough to hold more people than many small towns, several photographers asked me to pose, so I did. They informed me that the pictures would be available for purchase later. I had to shake my head, as I thought how much money I'd already paid yet they still weren't satisfied.

The ramp to the ship funneled all of the passengers who'd been cleared for boarding. I half expected to see Captain Stubing, Gopher, and Julie waiting to welcome me to the Love Boat. I had to laugh at myself when I spotted the real captain who towered over the rest of the crew and sported a full head of salt-and-pepper hair. He was handsome in a rugged sort of way, but he was no Captain Stubing—a man who could charm the socks off the guests and smile with his entire face while running a tight ship. This guy came across more intimidating, and he didn't appear to have time for cheerful small talk.

I was glad that my cruise-veteran friends had told me to have a bunch of small bills for tipping because so many people had their hands out for doing even the smallest task. I'd argued that I could give one massive tip once the cruise was over, but they insisted it was important to include small tips along the way if I wanted good service throughout the trip. I figured they were right since they had more experience.

I'd been warned that I might not be able to get to my cabin right away, at least not until the cleaning crew deemed it ready for occupancy. So I walked around and tried to figure out where everything was. The ship was big, and I'd heard that it wasn't full, but there still seemed to be quite a few people.

A couple of hours after I boarded, the cruise director announced over the PA that all of the cabins in my section of the ship were ready. As I walked down the corridor to my cabin, I couldn't help but smell the cleaning solution. It gave me a sense of comfort to know that they took cleanliness seriously.

When I finally got to my room, I panicked that my luggage wasn't there. So I went out to the hallway, where a sweet looking woman who appeared to be somewhere between Mama's and Nana's age ambled by.

She stopped and smiled at me. "Hello, dear. You look like you're lost."

I grinned back at her. "No, I'm just worried about my bags. They're not in my room."

"Oh, they'll be there shortly after dinner." She looked me up and down before meeting my gaze again. "I hope you brought something nice to wear in your carryon bag. We frown on sloppy attire in the dining room."

I grimaced. I'd brought all of my essentials, including a change of clothes, but it wasn't as nice as what I already had on. "I didn't—"

She flipped her hand from the wrist. "If you need something, you can just borrow it from me. I have more clothes than I'll ever be able to wear on this cruise."

"Thank you." No way would I even consider wearing anything this little old lady had in her closet, but I wasn't about to insult her.

She extended one of her tiny hands. "I don't believe I caught your name. I'm Betty Farber."

"Hi, Ms. Farber." When I took her hand, she crushed mine so hard tears burned my eyes. "My name is Autumn Spencer."

She gave me a beatific smile that belied her strength. "Please call me Betty."

"Okay. And you may call me Autumn."

"I wouldn't call you anything else." She lifted an eyebrow and then cackled. "I take it this is your first cruise."

"Yes." I paused and let out a nervous giggle. "I guess I'm pretty obvious."

She shrugged. "Everyone is when they first board. But give it a day or two, and you'll be a pro. Are you going to the party?"

"Party?"

She nodded. "The celebration when we pull away from the dock. It's fun. They have drinks and all kinds of noisemakers, and the view as we leave the dock is spectacular." She gave me a wink. "And after the party, I usually host an intimate little get-together in my cabin for a few close friends. Tonight I'll be serving my homemade cherry brandy. We crank up the music and dance the night away. You're welcome to join us."

"I think I'll pass." I'd never been into raucous parties, and this sounded a little too boisterous for my taste.

"Suit yourself. I can't imagine anyone wanting to miss it, but I'm sure you have your reasons."

"Have you done a lot of cruising?" I asked.

"That's all I do. I booked a series of cruises, came onboard, and I haven't left this ship in two years ... well, except when they make me get off to clean it, and that time they had to disinfect it a few months ago. I had to stay in a hotel for nearly a week." She rolled her eyes. "That was a hassle, but I think everything is under control now."

"You never leave the ship?"

She shook her head. "Like I said, I never leave the ship except when they make me."

"Do you go on any of the tours when we dock?"

She sneered at me. "What part of *never* don't you understand?" She rolled her eyes and clicked her tongue. "Some people are impossible."

"I'm sorry." This woman intimidated me.

"Don't be. You just have a lot to learn, and you're obviously tense about taking your first cruise." She turned slightly and gave me a narrow-eyed look. "Are you sure you don't want some of my homemade cherry brandy? It would relax you, and from what I can tell, you need a little loosening up."

Chapter 2

I went back into my cabin and thought about Betty. She seemed like a sweet woman, but there was something odd about her.

The more I pondered what she'd said about never having left the cruise ship, the more questions popped into my head. For example, she had to have a permanent address to have a passport, so what did she use? Did she have a family? And where did she go when she had to evacuate for cleaning—other than the time when they had to de-germ the boat a few months ago when she said she stayed in a hotel?

Dinner wasn't for a couple more hours, so I plopped down on my bed to get some rest. I stared up at the ceiling and let the thoughts swirl in my head. As much as I was looking forward to this vacation, a few doubts nipped at the back of my mind, and now I wasn't so sure it was a good idea to come alone. So far, all I'd seen once I got on the ship were couples and a few older people who didn't appear to want to be bothered ... and Betty Farber.

I closed my eyes for a little while, but after a few minutes, I started getting antsy. So I got up, glanced at the schedule, and decided to head on down to the dining area to check out what everyone else was wearing to make sure I didn't commit a serious dress code faux pas. I let out a sigh of relief when I realized I fit right in with my cruise-casual attire of white trousers, tank top, and floral overshirt. In fact, some of the people I encountered wore jeans. The only people who were dressed up were a few of the elderly women.

"Hey there, Miss."

I turned around at the sound of a man's voice and saw a couple about my parents' age standing behind me. "Hi."

"You look lost. Is there anything we can help you with?" The man glanced down at someone I assumed was his wife, who nodded, before looking back at me. "You remind us of our daughter, and I wouldn't want her to be as frightened as you look."

I forced my expression to soften. "I'm not frightened ... just a little bit overwhelmed. I've never been on a cruise before."

"Oh, we get it," the woman beside him said. "By the way, I'm Judith Bailey, and this is my husband Harvey. We do quite a bit of cruising, so if you have any questions, we're the ones to ask."

I introduced myself, and we started chatting about the fact that I was a teacher, and I needed to get away after being in a classroom all year with a bunch of seventh graders. "This is something I've always wanted to do."

They exchanged another glance, and then Mrs. Bailey smiled at me. "You're such a lovely young woman. I'm surprised you're not here with someone."

"I'm not married, and I couldn't get any of my friends to come along with me." The only person I'd asked was my best friend Bethany, and she just laughed at me. Her idea of a fun time was going to the mountains and camping out.

Someone came up to the couple, and they chatted while I awkwardly stood there looking around. I wasn't sure what to do—whether I should leave or wait until they finished talking to their friends. So I decided to stay, but I turned away slightly to give them some privacy.

As I watched everyone chatting with each other, my thoughts were all over the place. Mama had told me it wouldn't be too difficult to talk Summer into coming since she was always game for anything, and now I wished I'd taken her advice. As far as I knew, she still hasn't figured out what to do with her life. Her mother is Mama's sister, and I knew the two of them have been scheming ever since Summer left the police department, trying to help her do some career planning.

"Autumn?"

My attention snapped back to the couple. I smiled at Mrs. Bailey.

"Since tonight is casual with open seating, we wondered if you'd like to join us for dinner."

I nodded. "That would be nice if it's not an imposition."

"Of course it isn't. We'd much rather have dinner with a sweet young woman like you instead of some grouchy old lady who can't mind her own business."

"Or a crazy woman who keeps trying to push off some homemade booze," her husband added. "I can't help but wonder why she can't take *no* for an answer."

Those words alarmed me. I narrowed my gaze and realized they had their sights set on someone behind me. So I turned around and spotted Betty Farber approaching.

Betty looked at my new friends before cutting her gaze over at me. "Autumn, I told you that you could borrow something if your luggage didn't get to your cabin before dinner. You should have knocked on my door."

"I—"

Mrs. Bailey cackled. "Why on earth would she want to borrow one of your moth-eaten rags when she's perfectly dressed for the occasion?"

Whoa. These two obviously had a history, and it was clearly not a pleasant one.

"How on earth would you know anything about dressing for the occasion? I'll have you know my mother was one of the most elegant women in Boston, and she taught me manners that you'll never learn."

Mrs. Bailey's face turned red as she opened her mouth to respond, but her husband put his arm around her and pulled her back. He smiled at me. "Don't mind these two. They've been like this since the moment they met." He leaned over and whispered, "Not to mention their competitiveness."

His wife yanked herself away. "I am not competing with that woman."

Betty gave me a fake smile. "That's because she can't compete with me … on anything. Now would you like to go back to my cabin and find something appropriate for dinner?"

Before I had a chance to say a word, I was saved by one of the ship's crewmembers, announcing that we could enter the dining room. "There is no assigned seating tonight, so please choose a table quickly so everyone can be seated."

The crowd had grown so large I found myself being pushed along until we got inside the dining room. And then everyone zoomed toward a table. I wasn't sure what to do until Mrs. Bailey took hold of my arm and pulled me with her. Next thing I knew, I was sitting at a large round table with her, Mr. Bailey, and several other people they seemed to know.

Since I was the only inexperienced cruiser, I followed what the others did. Every now and then I caught my new friends watching me. When we made eye contact, they both smiled. It seemed sort of strange, but I figured it was their non-southern way of being friendly. Being from Nashville and hanging out with all my friends who were born and raised less than a couple of miles from me, I didn't have much experience with outsiders. Even my students, with few exceptions, were from Nashville. And now I was the outsider.

"So do you sing?" Mrs. Bailey asked.

I shook my head. "Not much. I don't have a great voice."

Mr. Bailey chuckled. "I thought everyone in Nashville sang ... at least that's what they make it look like on those TV shows. Do you like country music?"

"I do."

"So do we. Did you know there's a country music band playing in one of the lounges later? You're welcome to join us."

"I didn't know that." I pondered what to say since I now realized that drinking and hanging out in the lounges was one of the main activities on the cruise. "It's been a long day for me, so I think after dinner I'll just head on back to my cabin."

Mr. Bailey shrugged. "Suit yourself. I thought you might want to take advantage of all the wonderful things this cruise has to offer."

"Thank you, but I'll pass." I hoped these people wouldn't be so persistent about getting me to go to the lounge, or I'd spend half my trip trying to dodge them.

"Autumn, dear, I don't want to sound bossy or anything ..." Mrs. Bailey placed her hand on my arm. "But you're much too young to be spending a lot of time in your room." She made a sweeping motion with her hand. "There's a whole world of fun out there, waiting to be enjoyed. That's what cruising is all about."

Her husband nodded as he backed off his last comment and decided to chime in. "Yeah, there's a lot of fun to be had on this boat. I can't imagine anyone—especially such a pretty girl your age—wanting to sit around in the cabin."

"I ..." These were clearly partiers, and they would never understand someone like me. So I figured I might as well join them for a little while. I could have a soda and leave after a few songs. Maybe after that they'd leave me alone. "Well, okay, I suppose I can go for a little while."

"You'll have a blast. We do line dancing and sing along with the band. It is so much fun." Mrs. Bailey's eyes lit up as she spoke.

Dinner was good, but the conversation was so entertaining I couldn't think much about what I was eating. The people at my table had one cruise story after another—many of them leaving me in stitches.

"Eat up, Autumn. You'll need the energy." Mrs. Bailey shoveled another bite of chocolate cake into her mouth. She put down her fork and rubbed her hands together. "I can't wait to get you up on the dance floor. Harvey and I can show you some moves that'll knock your socks off."

An overwhelming feeling of dread washed over me. Mama had enrolled me in ballet when I was little, and after I stumbled over my own feet, the teacher actually told her I wasn't cut out for dance. I was relieved because I hated making a fool of myself. Now I knew I'd have a choice between coming across as a party pooper or showing everyone on the ship how uncoordinated I was.

I'd barely finished my dessert when Mr. Bailey

pointed to the door. "Look who just walked in."

I glanced over in the direction he was pointing and spotted a tall, middle-aged woman with flaming red hair and eyebrows so heavily drawn she appeared to be in a perpetual state of shock. "Who's that?" I asked.

"That woman—" Mrs. Bailey made a face and bobbed her head. "Her name is Aileen Graves, and she just happens to be the most hated person who has ever cruised the Caribbean."

Mr. Bailey leaned over, cupped his hand to one side of his mouth, and whispered, "She likes to flirt with all the men and then make them look like fools."

"Oh." This cruise was turning out to be way more than I'd bargained for.

Mrs. Bailey nodded. "And there's a rumor she murdered her husband, but no one can prove it."

Chapter 3

My ears rang, and my mouth went dry. I'd never met anyone suspected of killing anyone—let alone a spouse. It sounded really weird—like something you'd hear in a movie.

"Murdered her husband?" I looked at the woman and then at the rest of my tablemates. "Do y'all know her personally?"

"Only on the ship. We were here right before the fiasco when people died on the boat. There's even some speculation that she was responsible for that too."

"Do you really think so, Mrs. Bailey? I heard it was a supergerm."

"First of all, don't call me Mrs. Bailey. That makes me feel old. You can call us Judith and Harvey. And secondly, I don't for one minute think it was a germ that killed those people."

Some of the other passengers nodded and mumbled that they agreed. My stomach lurched.

Harvey shot his wife a warning look. "We probably shouldn't be talking like this with Autumn. I don't want to scare her."

"She needs to know these things. I'd feel awful if something happened, and we didn't warn her." She turned to me with a sympathetic smile. "If I were you, I wouldn't trust anyone I meet on a cruise ... except us, of course." She smiled lovingly at her husband. "Harvey, sweetheart, we have to look after her, just like we'd appreciate it if someone did that for one of our children."

Harvey made a face and nodded. "I suppose you're right, but we still don't need to frighten her."

Judith craned her neck to see Ms. Graves. "Look what she's doing now."

I looked but didn't notice anything out of the ordinary. But then some man approached, and she tilted her head back as she belted out laughter that was so loud we could hear it halfway across the noisy room. "Who's that man?" I asked.

"That's just it," Judith said. "I've never seen him before. She's doing what she always does, flirting with anyone who just happens to be close, never mind the fact that most of the men on this ship are married."

I never liked gossip, and this felt icky to me. The problem was I was curious and wanted to know more, which made me feel even worse.

Judith continued on her rant, until finally, Harvey stood up and helped his wife to her feet. "That's enough of this nonsense. Let's get outta here and go cut a rug in the lounge."

I remained sitting there for a few seconds, stunned by how he could talk about dancing right after his wife told me they thought there was a murderer in our midst. Harvey pulled my chair back.

I slowly stood. "Thanks." My voice squeaked, so I cleared my throat. "I really don't—"

"C'mon, Autumn." Judith linked arms with me and led me out of the dining room. "It'll be fun. I love sharing this stuff with first-timers. You'll have so much fun you won't ever want to leave."

The cruise ship captain passed us on the way to the lounge. "Welcome aboard." The sound of his booming voice coupled with his overpowering ruggedness made me wish I were invisible. He flashed a flirty smile in Judith's direction. "Is this your daughter?"

Judith gave the captain a playful swat. "You know better that that, Captain Myers. This is Autumn. We just met her this evening."

The captain grinned at me, this time in a softer manner. "I'm glad you met someone who knows the ropes. Have fun, you three. Let Jerome or Andrea know if you need anything."

After we passed him and he was out of hearing distance, I spoke up. "Who are Jerome and Andrea?"

"Jerome Pratt is the purser, and Andrea Zeller is the new cruise director. We were on her first voyage right after the ship started sailing again," Harvey explained. "Neither of them does a great job, but I'm sure they'll get better over time. Anyway, it's their jobs to make sure all the passengers are taken care of and having a good time."

Judith nodded. "And the purser is responsible for the money."

I never realized a cruise was so complicated, but it made sense. With all of this new information swirling in my head, I followed Judith and Harvey to the lounge where the music was loud, and the partiers were even louder. I hesitated at the door, but Harvey laughed and pulled me inside.

He pointed to a two-seater table in the corner. "Let's grab that table before someone else does. You and Judith go on ahead and claim it, while I find another chair."

For me, the next hour and a half was a miserable, delicate balance of trying to be polite and wishing I was anywhere but in the lounge. For Judith and Harvey, it was clearly loads of fun. They laughed as they pulled me up for a line dance in a space that wasn't nearly big enough for the couple dozen or so people trying to bust a few dance moves. At least my klutziness didn't seem so bad since everyone was bumping into and stepping all over each other.

After a while, I couldn't deal with it anymore, and I decided to call it a night. It had been long enough that I didn't think it would be rude to excuse myself. Judith and Harvey both gave me a hug, holding onto me until I promised I'd look for them again. Then I darted out of that lounge as quickly as my legs would carry me.

When I finally got to my cabin, I ran inside, closed the door behind me, and leaned against the wall. I looked around the room and saw that my luggage had finally made it, just as Betty had told me it would. That was a relief. I hated the thought of having to deal with the hassles of trying to track it down. One of my friends had that happen, and she said it was a couple of days into the trip when she finally got her stuff. Apparently, someone had it in their cabin, but they kept forgetting to tell the ship's staff.

I changed into my pajamas and brushed my teeth. My head still pounded with the rhythm from the music in the lounge, and I doubted I'd be able to go to sleep right away. So I reached into my carryon bag and pulled out my e-reader.

It took a while to clear out my ears and my head. I finally fell asleep shortly after midnight. Although I had one crazy dream after another, I managed to stay asleep until morning.

What sounded like cattle stampeding past my door startled me awake early the next morning. I sat up momentarily, but a short burst of vertigo caused me to quickly flop back in the bed. What on earth was going on out there?

I took a couple of deep breaths before attempting to sit up again. The noise stopped, so I got up and walked across the room. After only a brief hesitation, I unlocked the door and pulled it open a couple of inches to take a look.

All I saw was one person pacing. She must have heard me because she spun around and stared right at me.

"Betty?"

The glazed look in her eyes concerned me, so I

took a chance and stepped out into the hallway, in spite of the fact that I was still in my pajamas. She blinked a couple of times, but she never looked away.

"Are you okay?" She clearly wasn't, so I amended my comment. "What happened?"

She slowly shook her head, turned around, and went back into the room a couple of doors down, leaving me standing there, wondering what on earth was going on.

I started back to my room, when I heard the sound of pounding footsteps again. This was too weird. I had no idea what was happening, and once again, I wondered why I thought this cruise was a good idea. I'd booked it because I needed rest and relaxation, but so far it was anything but restful ... or relaxing.

Even though I was curious as all get out, I didn't want to hang out in the hallway in my pajamas. So I went back into my cabin and closed the door. I went over to my handbag and pulled out my phone, but once I woke it up, I realized that if I was able to get service out here on the open water, my roaming charges would be through the roof. My friends had warned me about this, but I really wanted to talk to someone back home. Someone sane. Someone who loved me.

I sat down on the edge of my bed to ponder my situation. The sound of hollering down the hall grew louder as more people made their way outside their cabins. My breathing had become shallow, so I concentrated on taking several deep breaths, inhaling to the count of four and slowly blowing it out to the count of eight.

Whatever was happening outside the cabin was obviously not good. In fact, it might have been a tragedy for all I knew. With this ship's history and from all the stories I heard last night, it could be anything.

My body was already tense before I began this trip, but now I was so anxious I thought I might explode. Being in a classroom with a bunch of hormonal seventh graders didn't seem so bad at the moment, and I found myself wishing that was where I was.

After a couple of deep, cleansing breaths, I knew I couldn't just sit here and worry. I needed to get out of this room and find out what was going on.

It took me about twenty minutes to shower, brush my teeth, get dressed, and make myself presentable. The volume of the voices had subsided, but I could still hear people milling about out in the corridor.

I placed my hand on the doorknob but hesitated to open the door as my mind began to tick off some of the possibilities. Maybe someone had been hurt. Or there could be a robber out there mugging people. Or worse ...

Before I gathered the nerve to pull the door open, someone knocked. My eyes twitched.

"Autumn, are you in there?" It sounded like Betty.

"Yes."

"Then will you please open the door? There's something you need to know."

Chapter 4

Against better judgment, I let Betty into my cabin. Her wild-eyed expression startled me, but I tried not to let her notice.

"You might want to stay here in your cabin for a few hours," she said. "All kinds of you-know-what is breaking loose out there."

"I heard. What's that all about?" I gestured toward the sofa. "Have a seat."

"I think I'll stand. This is making me all jittery."

I lowered myself onto the edge of the corner chair. "Do you know what happened?"

She held her arms out and gestured with her palms up. "I can't give you the details, but I do know that there's been an attempted murder."

"Attempted murder?" Goosebumps rippled over my body as I remembered what Judith and Harvey had said about that woman, Aileen, possibly murdering her husband. "Are you sure?"

Betty glanced down and nodded. "I'm pretty sure.

It takes a while for the cops to get here since they have to fly someone in on a helicopter."

"Doesn't this ship have law enforcement?" My throat constricted, so I coughed and took a deep breath. "There has to be some sort of protection."

"Well ..." Betty began to pace and acting even stranger than before. "They do have people who call themselves law enforcement, but I've been watching them for the past couple of years. If someone wants to do something bad, it's really not that difficult if they know what they're doing. The law enforcement folks onboard have their hands tied since there's nowhere to take the criminal."

I sank back in the chair and thought about what she'd just said, and then I thought about Mama's request for me to ask Summer to join me. Once again, regret about not inviting my cousin washed over me. She'd know what to do.

"Do you know how the person was ..." I cleared my throat again. "How he was almost murdered?"

"She. The victim is a woman."

My eyes bugged. "Do you know who it is?"

Betty pursed her lips and nodded. "Yes, unfortunately, I do."

"Who?"

"Aileen Graves."

That shot Judith and Harvey's theory out of the water ... at least I thought it did. "Do you have any idea who might have done it?"

Betty's face changed. "Could have been anyone. I don't think there's anyone here who'll miss her if she doesn't make it." She glanced down at her feet before raising her gaze back to mine. "I felt sorry for her since no one would talk to her during dinner, so I invited her to my cabin." Betty shrugged. "But she didn't stay long. Next thing I know, someone's trying to kill her."

"It's so sad." I paused. "And scary."

"Why do you think it's scary?"

"You don't think it's scary that someone was almost murdered on this ship that you're stuck on for a week?"

"Not really. I've been here long enough to know this isn't all that common … and it has nothing to do with me, although it is a terrible inconvenience."

"Inconvenience?" I didn't even try to hold back the shrillness in my voice.

"Yes, inconvenience. When something this big happens onboard, all the ship crewmembers turn their attention toward that instead of trying to make it an enjoyable experience for the rest of us."

"But what about those people who died from the germs a few months ago? Do you think—?"

"You worry too much, Autumn. This is your vacation. You're supposed to be relaxing."

I looked directly at Betty who held my gaze for a couple of seconds before looking away again. She was acting strange, one minute telling me to stay in my cabin so I'd stay safe to telling me I worried too much.

"So what do you think will happen now?" I asked.

"Who knows? I've seen people die and get sick on the ship before, but this is the first known attempted murder case I've been involved with."

Involved with? What a strange thing for her to have said. I wanted to ask her about it, but her behavior made me think I wouldn't get a straight answer.

Betty moved toward the door. "Stay in your cabin for a couple of hours, Autumn, and then it'll probably be safe to go out."

"Maybe after I get something to eat. I'm hungry."

"Then have something delivered." Without another word, she walked out and pulled the door closed behind her.

All kinds of alarm bells went off in my head. She'd used some interesting phrases, almost making it seem as though she knew more than she was letting on. But what could she know? She was a little old lady who had nothing better to do with her life than live on a ship and interfere in the lives of other guests.

I wanted to smack myself for being so hard on Betty. I'd never been a mean girl, and I certainly didn't want to start now. After all, most people had reasons for being the way they were, and something might have happened to her to cause her to be the way she was. I needed to have nicer thoughts about someone who was at least making an effort to be my friend and maybe even protect me ... although her attempts were awkward at best.

I decided to take Betty's advice and order something to be brought up. I picked up the limited room service menu and chose a few things that sounded good and would tide me over until I could get out and visit one of the buffets everyone raved about.

Once I knew what I wanted, I picked up the phone and punched in the number at the bottom of the menu. It rang a dozen times, and no one picked up. So I put the receiver back in the cradle, walked over to the door, and cracked it open.

There stood Betty, shaking her finger at me. "Get back inside, girlie. I told you to have something delivered."

"But—"

Commotion at the other end of the hall caught both of our attention. She shuffled in that direction as she muttered something about how people doing stupid things could get them killed. I backed into my room, shut the door, and locked it.

I went to the phone and tried again to place an order, this time letting it ring more than twenty times … still no answer. And no answering machine. I sighed. And then my stomach let out a loud gurgling sound, reminding me it was past time to put something in it.

I waited a few more minutes before getting my cross-body bag and heading out the door in spite of Betty's warnings. I figured if I was going to die, it would be much better on a full stomach.

Fortunately, Betty wasn't anywhere in sight this time. And I realized the commotion wasn't coming from an attempted murderer. It was a family traveling with four rambunctious, pre-adolescent boys who didn't seem to care that they were disturbing other passengers.

The mother appeared worn down as she gave me an apologetic look. My heart went out to her. I was able to take a couple of months away from the kids I taught, while she had at least eighteen years with no break—unless she had a job outside the home. Some people didn't realize that going to work was often less trouble than staying home with the kids. And going on a cruise with them? I wondered what on earth that mom was thinking.

When I got to the deck where the buffet was, I noticed that there was food out, but no one was getting anything. In fact, there were only a few people on the deck, and they were all resting on lounge chairs. That was odd. It looked like a nice spread.

I walked around a little bit, until I ran into someone who clearly worked for the cruise line. "When does the breakfast buffet start?"

"It already started." She gave me a brief glance and then scurried away.

My stomach growled again, only much louder this time, so I figured I might as well go ahead and fill up a plate with food. Once I had fruit, cheese, a couple of muffins, and a variety of other delicious looking foods piled high on my plate, I walked over to a table topped by a humongous rainbow-striped umbrella. I never minded eating alone, but it would have been nice to have someone to talk to this morning.

The fruit was deliciously cold and sweet. The muffins were okay, but I made a mental note to choose something else next time.

"Hi, Autumn. Are you sure you want to eat that?"

I glanced over my shoulder as the voice drew closer. "Hi, Judith. I was starving."

"Harvey and I were too, but we didn't want to risk getting poisoned."

"Poisoned?" My throat constricted.

"Yes, poisoned." She pulled out a chair across the table and plopped down. "Don't tell me you haven't heard about Aileen getting poisoned."

I looked down at my plate that was now half empty, and a completely different feeling washed over me. "Um ... I did hear that someone tried to murder her, but I didn't realize she'd been poisoned."

"Yeppers. She ate something last night that they're pretty sure contained cyanide, and somehow she managed to call Doc Healey before it was too late. He took care of her right away." She made a face. "I think he induced vom—"

Harvey interrupted her. "I think she gets the picture, Judith. You don't have to go into graphic detail."

"How did he know it was cyanide?"

Judith contorted her mouth as she shrugged. "He's a doctor. I guess they just know those things."

My cheeks puffed as I blew out a breath. I looked back at my plate and then at Judith. "Well, I've already consumed a little bit of everything the buffet had to offer, and so far so good."

"That's nice." Judith gave me a beatific smile. "Maybe I'll get something. That bagel we had delivered to the room was stale."

"I tried to have something delivered, but they didn't answer when I called."

"Same here," Harvey said. "That's why I went to

the desk and told them what we wanted."

I wasn't able to take another bite of my food, now that I knew about the cyanide poisoning, so I just sat there and stared at the deck as I waited for Judith to return. She had a banana and a couple of boiled eggs on the plate and a couple of bottles of water in the crook of her elbow.

She grinned at me. "Trying to watch my figure. I totally blew it last night."

Judith had a nice figure for a woman her age, so I made a mental note to be more careful with my own diet in the future. "What else do you know about the attempted murder?"

She shrugged, almost as though we were talking about something as innocuous as the weather. "Basically just what I told you. It was a matter of time before someone went after Aileen. That bag is horrible. No one can stand her." She peeled back the skin on the top part of her banana and shoved it into her mouth. "Mmm, this is so delicious. I wish I could find fruit this good back home."

"Where is back home?"

"North Carolina. My husband and I moved there from Ohio where the winters are brutal. We bought a small bungalow where we retired. It's a quick plane ride to the cruise ships. Sometimes we leave out of Miami, but occasionally we go on cruises out of Tampa. We're thinking we might go on an Alaskan cruise next time, but we'd have to fly to Seattle." She paused and put down her fork. "Harvey wanted to do that this time, but I talked him out of it because I wasn't in the mood to fly that far. I wish I'd given in ..." She smiled at me. "But that wouldn't have been as exciting, now, would it?"

The look she cast in my direction made me shiver. Exciting? I would have given up an exciting attempt at murder on a Caribbean cruise any day for a chance to go on a peaceful Alaskan cruise.

Now that she'd mentioned her husband, I looked around and saw that he was nowhere in sight. "Speaking of Harvey, where is he?"

Chapter 5

There was a split second of hesitation before she responded. "He had an appointment for a massage."

A massage sounded good to me, so I made a mental note to try to book one. "It must be nice to be able to go on so many cruises."

She glanced away momentarily before looking at me and gave a half nod. "Most of the time, it is, but I have to admit I sometimes get cabin fever. Harvey tells me I need to get off the ship more when we stop at ports, but I don't like walking all over creation, just to have all those people trying to sell me stuff I don't need."

"What people are trying to sell you stuff?"

"You know …" She stopped herself and gave me a condescending smile. "Oh, that's right. This is your first cruise, so you don't know. When we get to the various ports, there are hundreds of people waiting for the suckers on the ship to get off so we'll spend perfectly good money for the junk they have." She leaned forward and whispered as though there was anyone around to hear her. "They say they made it themselves, but sometimes they forget to peel off the *made in China* tags.

"I was hoping to take one of the tours, but maybe that's not such a good idea."

She shrugged. "Suit yourself. If you enjoy walking around and getting all sweaty in tourist traps, you might like it. At any rate, I like to have some time to myself, so when Harvey goes off on his merry way, I stick around the cabin and read." She pulled a Kindle out of her bag. "This is the best invention known to mankind. I have more than a hundred books in here, all waiting for me to immerse myself in their make-believe worlds of love and romance while my husband does his thing."

"So you like romance novels?"

"I do." She laced her fingers together. "How about you? Do you like to read?"

I nodded. "I like romance novels, but right now I'm into mysteries. It's fun to try to solve them."

Her expression instantly changed. "Don't tell me you're an amateur sleuth."

"Oh, not in real life ... just when I read the books."

"Are you any good at it?" The lines on her forehead deepened as she gave me a concerned look. "I mean, do you always solve the mystery?"

"Most of the time I figure out who committed the crime if the clues are strong enough, but occasionally I get it wrong."

Judith's jaw tightened as she shoved away from

the table. "I'd better go see about Harvey. He should be back in the cabin by now."

Before I had a chance to say another word, she was gone. And I was alone again.

Her reaction startled me, but I noticed from the very beginning that she was an odd bird. I hadn't touched my food since she'd first joined me, and when I glanced back at it, I wasn't nearly as hungry as I was when I first sat down.

The sun was shining, but the wind kept the deck cool. Back home, I would have had to stay inside in the air conditioning to be this comfortable. There was something special about an ocean breeze.

A few people had returned and strolled by—some of them acknowledging me with a smile and others acting as though I was invisible. But I didn't care. They could do whatever they wanted to do. All I wanted was to relax.

I noticed that as people started to come out, the lounge chairs began filling up quickly. So I got up and found one that was somewhat hidden in a little alcove so I could have some privacy for my own thoughts—and maybe a nap.

Before I had a chance to settle back, someone else approached, and this time it was the captain. "You left early last night. I hope you are enjoying your time on the ship." He leaned against the rail. "You are, aren't you?"

I smiled. "I haven't exactly had a chance to yet." Since he didn't bring up what seemed to be on everyone else's mind, I decided to. "How is the lady who was poisoned?"

A frown quickly replaced his smile. "Who told you someone was poisoned?"

No point in getting anyone in trouble, and based on his expression, I thought that might be the case. "Just people talking. Is she …" I grimaced. "Is she conscious?"

He nodded. "She might have eaten some rotten food …" His lips tightened momentarily. "Before she boarded the ship, of course."

"Yes, of course."

The captain pulled away from the railing. "I'm sure she'll be just fine. Doc Healey is taking excellent care of her until her health improves or we can get her to a hospital at the first port of call."

"But I thought—" I stopped myself before divulging that I'd already spoken to Betty about what happened and how the authorities were supposed to arrive by helicopter. "I hope she gets better quickly."

The captain glanced down at something on his belt, and I saw that it was some sort of communication device. "I need to get back to the machine room. If there's anything you need, let Andrea Zeller know." He forced a smile, but his eyes didn't crinkle as I'd seen last night when he appeared truly happy. "She's the cruise director, and it's her job to make sure everyone enjoys their time on the ship. Unfortunately, I didn't have a say in hiring her." His jaw tightened momentarily. "If she gives you any trouble, let me know. I'd like to replace her and that lousy purser as soon as possible. I don't know what the company thought they were doing when they brought in two inexperienced crewmembers." He shook his head as he walked away mumbling something I couldn't understand.

After he left, I leaned back again and closed my eyes, hoping to have a little quiet time. But I was awakened by a splash of water. I opened my eyes in time to see a little boy who appeared to be about seven or eight being chased by a boy who looked like he might be around twelve, the same age as the ones in my classes. They both had squirt guns, but the smaller child had a look of fear written all over his face.

I popped right up. "Whoa. Slow down, guys."

The little boy did what I told him to, which made it easier for the older one to catch him. When I realized I'd just handicapped the younger one, I hopped up out of my chair and jumped between them.

"Move, lady. We're playing cops and robbers." The older of the two children issued a defiant look, and I wasn't about to let him get away with it.

"You were playing cops and robbers until you squirted me. That's when the game changed." I planted a fist on my hip, teacher style. "Do your parents know where you are?"

"We're not supposed to talk to strangers." He tried to dart around me, but I was too fast for him, which obviously surprised him.

"Too bad. You should have thought about that before you doused *this* stranger with water."

He looked me in the eyes and scowled. "I told you to move."

"Would you like to rephrase that?"

"Move."

"I don't move unless I'm asked politely," I said, holding his gaze.

He rolled his eyes. "Move, please."

I glanced around, hoping there would be another adult nearby who might have witnessed this. But I didn't see one, so I stepped aside.

"Don't let this happen again, or I'll have to have a talk with your parents."

They both gave me one last quick glance before continuing their chase. Now I realized the little boy was just as scrappy as his older brother, but that still didn't give them the right to squirt people trying to relax.

I leaned back and closed my eyes again, but my nerves that were already on edge now felt raw and blistered. All it took was the sound of a woman's shrill voice to send me over the edge. I looked in the direction of the voice and saw a woman holding the two boys by the arms and screeching at them. I wanted to scream, but being the mannerly southern woman I'd been taught to be, I didn't. Instead, I stood up, stretched, and headed for my cabin.

Once I got to the hallway leading to my room, I spotted the ship's purser leaving Betty's cabin. I thought that was odd, but I also remembered the fact that this had been her home for a couple of years, so I figured they had some business to take care of.

.

Chapter 6

Betty stepped out into the hallway and looked directly at me. "I thought I heard someone coming. What are you doing out there all by yourself?"

I hated having to explain anything, but again, I didn't want to be rude. "I had to get out for a little while."

She scowled. "I hope you didn't do too much talking."

"Too much talking?" I narrowed my eyes and gave her a curious look. "About what?"

"About what you know."

"What I know about what?" I asked.

"The murder ... I mean the attempted murder. It's supposed to be a secret."

"I really don't think it's much of a secret. You know, I know, and—" I caught myself before I mentioned Judith's name. There wasn't any point in bringing someone else into Betty's world of drama.

"And what?" Betty tilted her head and gave me an

accusatory look. "Who did you tell?"

I lifted both hands and shook my head as I stepped farther away from this woman who was appearing crazier by the minute. "I didn't tell a soul."

"How do I know you didn't talk?" Her voice cracked.

I edged closer to my cabin as slowly as I could so I wouldn't get her any more worked up than she already was. "I reckon you'll just have to take my word for it." As soon as I got to the door, I unlocked it and put one foot inside. "I'll talk to you later, Betty. I need some rest."

Once inside my room, I shuddered—something I found myself doing quite a bit since I'd been on this ship. Having a cabin in the same vicinity as Betty wasn't working out for me, and it seemed to upset her as well. So I picked up the phone and requested a different room, only to be told the ship was full, and there wasn't anything else available. I knew the ship wasn't full, and when I mentioned it, she became extremely defensive, letting me know that was none of my business. I could tell she wasn't going to be any help at all.

"Is there anything else we can help you with?" The woman's instant change to her over-the-top perky voice reminded me of the noisy squirrels outside my old bedroom window at Mama and Daddy's house. "Would you like to purchase one of the super fun excursions at St. Thomas?"

"No, that's okay."

"If you change your mind or decide to add more

adventures to your agenda, don't hesitate to call back. We want our passengers to have a wonderful trip and one you'll always remember."

"It would be a much more wonderful trip if—"

"As I told you …" She'd switched back to her cranky voice. "Like I said, the ship is full, and we don't have a vacant room to put you in."

"Okay." I sighed. "Thank you anyway." I dropped the phone back into the cradle and pondered what she'd said. This was definitely not a wonderful trip so far, but it was one I'd always remember.

A knock came at my door a few minutes later. "Who is it?"

"Harvey Bailey. I'd like to talk to you."

I crossed the room and opened the door a couple of inches. I'd barely met this man, and it didn't seem appropriate to have him come into my room. "Did you need something?"

"Mind if I come in?" He stuck his foot in the door, so if I closed it, I knew it might hurt. But still …

"Can we talk later?" I glanced over my shoulder and pretended to speak to someone. Before I had a chance to turn back to face him, he'd shoved the door open, pushing me off balance and farther into the room. Next thing I knew, he was in my room, with the door closed behind him.

"You know my wife is crazy, right?" His eyes had taken on a creepy glow, so if I hadn't been scared to begin with, I was now.

As it was, nothing came out of my mouth when I opened it. Well, nothing but a squeak.

"I want you to stay away from her unless I'm around."

I swallowed hard and managed a slight grunt. "Uh ..."

"If you don't, you'll be sorry."

"Okay." I glanced at the door, wishing he'd leave. The very thought of what he might do next had me sweating.

He lifted his hands in the air and let them flop back to his sides. "You are obviously clueless."

"About what?"

"See? That's what I'm talking about. You don't even know what's right in front of you." He took a step backward toward the door. "Let's keep it that way, shall we?"

Again, I swallowed, hoping to catch my breath but knowing that wouldn't happen until he was gone. Once again, I mentally beat myself up, reminding myself once again that I should have listened to Mama about inviting Summer. She'd know exactly what to do, and Harvey wouldn't stand a chance.

Harvey finally decided to give up on whatever he was trying to intimidate me with. "You'd better do as I said," he reminded me. "Don't do anything stupid, or you'll regret it."

I nodded as I made a mental note to stay as far away from him and his wife as humanly possible on this ship. He locked gazes with me one last time before he turned and left, pulling the door closed behind him.

As soon as my legs stopped wobbling, I ran to the door and locked it again, although I wondered why I bothered with that since I kept opening it to people. And then I sank to the floor and buried my face in my hands. I was more than twice as tense and anxious as I was when I started the cruise, and we weren't even one-third of the way finished with it.

I remained sitting on the floor as I pondered what to do next. It took a while, but I finally came to a conclusion. Since this cruise wasn't giving me what I needed, I'd find a way to go home early. In the meantime, I'd avoid other people and get as much rest as possible. A settling feeling came over me as I realized how relaxing being home in my own apartment would be, without the obligations of work and everyday life. A stay-cation was exactly what I needed. Too bad I hadn't figured that out before spending all my money on this trip.

With my mind made up, I changed into a fresh outfit and went out for a stroll on the deck to clear my mind. A few more people were out—mostly couples strolling hand in hand, looking as though they didn't have a care in the world. I wondered whether or not they knew about the attempted murder and eventually figured they didn't … or they wouldn't be out and about looking as though nothing mattered.

I was scheduled for early dinner seating, but I decided to have my food delivered to my cabin instead. So I went to the desk to request that. The woman shook her head. "Unfortunately, it's too late, and we're short staffed on this cruise." She gave me an apologetic look. "I'm sorry."

"Can you tell me who else is at my table?"

"Sure, let me pull that up." After she read off the list of the names, I figured it would be fine since I didn't know any of them.

I went back to my cabin to wait until time to go. I put on something a little bit nicer but avoided anything with too much color since I wanted to blend in.

I approached the dining room with some trepidation, hoping I wouldn't see Harvey and Judith. Fortunately, everyone at my table had a friendly face, and I didn't see any of the people I wanted to avoid.

The food was delicious. Friends back home had warned me that it was easy to overindulge, so I ordered half portions of a couple of courses and skipped some of the offerings.

"Go ahead and have some more." The woman next to me leaned over and gave me an earnest look. "It doesn't cost extra unless you order mixed drinks."

"I know, but I don't want to be stuffed."

The man she was with—the guy I assumed was her husband—laughed. "We blew our budget to come on this cruise, so I told Amanda to gorge herself since we'll probably starve after we get home."

His wife nodded and made a face. "Our grocery budget is shot for the next year … or more."

This drew laughter from everyone around the table as they nodded their understanding. I smiled to be polite, but I still didn't want to eat too much. I had some planning to do later, after I got back to my room.

"I could never do what you're doing," Amanda said.

I tilted my head. "What's that?"

"Go on a cruise all by myself." She grimaced. "It seems scary."

Her husband lifted his chin and puffed out his chest. "She needs a big, strong bodyguard to protect her." He jutted his chin a couple of inches. "And that's where I come in."

"Yeah, James has always been such a good protector. We started dating back in high school, after some guys acted like jerks to me. After we got together, no one ever did that again." She reached out and took his hand. "And now I would never go anywhere without him."

The other women at the table agreed with Amanda, but the only other single person at the table, a guy who appeared slightly older than me, wearing a suit and an extra skinny tie grinned at me. "I think it says a lot for Autumn to do this all alone. I like strong women."

I wasn't sure if he was coming to my defense to be kind or if he was flirting with me. He seemed nice, but I totally wasn't interested in him. His expression let me know he had other thoughts.

James lifted a finger. "Hey, I have an idea. Why don't the two of you get together? That way, you don't have to—" He jumped as though Amanda might have kicked him under the table. He gave her a pained look. "I'm just sayin'."

"If they want to get together, it's up to them, sweetie." Amanda cast an understanding glance in my direction before turning back to her husband. "It's not our place to match make. We're on our honeymoon."

That started a whole new conversation about why they'd want to dine with so many other people while honeymooning. "If I were you, I'd stay in my cabin and have room service," one of the other men said.

Conversation throughout the rest of dinner continued along the same lines, so I was glad when it was time for dessert. I requested a single scoop of sherbet just to keep anyone from thinking I was being antisocial or dieting. I finished half of it before excusing myself and heading back to my cabin.

I'd no sooner shut the door and locked it when I heard a knock. My heart jumped, and my stomach lurched.

"Autumn, I know you're in there. It's me, Judith. I need to talk to you. It's urgent."

Harvey's warning rang in my head. I didn't want to open the door, but she sounded desperate.

Chapter 7

After a moment of gut-clenching trepidation, I slowly opened the door and let Judith in. The look on her face was completely different from the last time I saw her. Instead of a playful expression, she was wild-eyed and flushed.

"You need to stay away from my husband." The words tumbled out of her mouth so quickly it took a few seconds to register.

"I—"

She held up her hands to stop me. "I'm not saying you're doing anything wrong." A snort escaped as she continued. "After all, you're a beautiful young woman, and he's a dried up old has-been, so I don't think you're after anything of his. He doesn't even have a big bank account to offer someone like you."

This was just weird. I had no idea what to say or if I should say anything. So I just kept my mouth shut.

"Something is going on with him, and ..." She looked around as though she thought someone else might be able to hear, and then she lowered her voice. "I'm worried that he might have been the one who poisoned Aileen."

"That's a strong statement for someone to be making about her own husband." I took a step back. "Do you have any proof?"

She shook her head. "No, but he's given me enough clues to make me think he could have." She frowned. "Not saying he did it for certain, though, so don't run out and tell anyone. I just wanted to let you know that I think he's capable of doing it, so you need to be very careful."

"Are you afraid for your safety?"

"Not really. I would never eat or drink anything he brings me."

"But the two of you seem—"

"I put on an act so he doesn't get all weird." She stuck out her bottom lip and blew, lifting her bangs from her forehead. "It's not easy."

She wouldn't have convinced me that Harvey might have tried to murder someone if he hadn't pushed his way into my cabin and scared me into deciding to leave. But I didn't dare tell her that.

"You probably want to know why I suspect him, don't you?"

I looked at her, but I was afraid to say anything. So I just gave a brief nod.

"Well, first of all, his first impression of Aileen changed so quickly, I'm thinking something must have happened. He thought she was a sweet person ..." Judith rolled her eyes. "Why he thought that, I'll never understand. She was always crass and rude. Anyway, one night he went down to the casino, and when he came back ... hoo boy, he was on a rant. He couldn't stop talking about what a hag she was."

"That doesn't mean he wants to kill her."

Judith looked down at the floor and sighed before meeting my gaze. "There's more."

I really didn't want to hear more, but it didn't look like I had much of a choice, unless I ordered her to leave my cabin. And no matter how much her presence annoyed me, I had to admit I was curious.

"A couple of times, I found things in his pockets after our cruises ... like a color of lipstick I would never wear." Her eyes misted over. "I'm almost certain it was Aileen's."

"What makes you think it was hers?"

"It's the same shade of fuchsia she always wears." She let out a little hiccup. "Once when she finished eating, I saw her apply her lipstick, and it was in the same black tube with the gold trim as what I found in his pocket."

That did seem suspicious to me too, but I wasn't about to tell her that. Instead, I remained quiet, hoping she'd run out of steam so I could have a little time to figure out what I needed to do next.

Judith rambled on and on about the different things that made her think something was going on between her husband and Aileen—from the fact that she was always on the same cruise ship, regardless of where they went, to seeing the looks they gave each other.

"But I thought he said she was a hag," I countered.

"That's only recently. I'm thinking she might have told him to buzz off, and it damaged his ego."

The memory of him pushing his way into my cabin returned again, and I felt sick to my stomach. If he'd tried to kill someone, I needed to avoid him at all costs. But then he'd told me his wife was dangerous. If I had to choose one to believe, at this point, it would probably be Judith.

"Why are you telling me all of this?" I asked.

"Trust me, I didn't want to, but you're the only one I've met who doesn't have a history with any of us, and I'd like to protect you. And for some strange reason, I feel like I can trust you." She shrugged. "Maybe it's because you're a schoolteacher. I always thought teachers were the smartest, most trustworthy people alive."

"I don't know about that." I thought about several teachers I didn't trust, but I didn't think now was the time to bring it up. "I'm thinking you need to talk to someone who can actually do something."

Judith folded her arms as a scowl formed on her face, highlighting all the wrinkles around her eyes and mouth. Until now, I thought she was attractive and youthful looking for her age, but this wasn't a good expression for her. "Like who?"

"Like maybe the captain or someone in law enforcement?"

She leaned back and cackled. "You're kidding, right?" Before I had a chance to answer, she shook her head. "The captain isn't any better than my husband. If

I didn't think Harvey might have done it, I would place my bets on the captain."

Now I'd heard it all. "The captain? Why on earth would someone in his position do something so … so horrible?"

"You sure are naïve for a woman in your …" Her voice trailed off as she squinted at me. "How old did you say you were?"

"I'm in my thirties."

She flicked her hand from the wrist. "There ya go. When I was your age, I was married and had two kids. I'd been around the block enough by then, I knew what was going on." Then she planted her fists on her hips and bobbed her head. "So I suppose it's time to give you a lesson in human nature. There are people in high authority who use their positions to lord over us. They chew you up and spit you out. They do whatever they can to intimidate those they consider weak, and they'll stop at nothing to get what they want."

"So you're saying the captain would think it's okay to kill—or attempt to kill someone?"

Judith blew out what sounded like a breath of exasperation. "You really don't get it, do you?" She rolled her eyes and continued. "It's not that he thinks it's okay. It's more of a case of thinking he's entitled to do whatever he wants because he's in a position of power."

"Oh." I hated being talked to like a child, but she was obviously out of her mind. The stress and anger had clearly gotten to her … and maybe she was as crazy as her husband said she was.

"You don't believe me, do you?" She smirked. "I bet you still think the captain is beyond reproach. You probably believe he's some super hero whose sole mission in life is to make all his passengers safe and happy." Her eyes bugged as she shoved her finger into my chest. "But that isn't at all how it is with him. He thinks he's God's gift to women, and they don't have any rights whatsoever."

Whoa. I couldn't imagine what made her so angry with the captain of this ship. Her husband, I understood because of the jealousy factor, but the captain? Then it dawned on me. Maybe there was jealousy over him too. But of course I didn't dare say that.

Judith's demeanor changed again, only now she appeared somewhat contrite. "I probably shouldn't have come here and unloaded on you, but there's something about you that makes me feel protective." She gave me a half smile. "I'm also comfortable around you. There's a sweetness about you that gives me the feel-goods."

Okay, now I felt bad for her, but I still took a step back in case she decided to act on her *feel-goods* and give me a hug or something. "Thank you."

"I guess I'd better leave now." She took a couple of steps toward the door, stopped and turned around to face me. "Just be careful, okay? I'd hate for anything to happen to you."

"I'll be careful."

"And don't tell a soul a word I said. If you do, I'll deny it."

With that, she left the cabin and closed the door. I shut my eyes, took a deep breath, and slowly let it out. This cruise was turning out to be the weirdest experience in my life.

I was about to lock the cabin door when I heard another knock. My first reaction was to pretend I wasn't in, but what if it was important?

This time, I spoke before opening it. "Who is it?"

"Your neighbor Betty Farber. Can we talk?"

I opened the door and saw her standing in the hallway, shivering. So I stepped aside and gestured toward my room. "Come on in."

She stepped inside and spun around to face me. "Did I see Judith Bailey leave your cabin a few minutes ago?"

I hesitated for a moment before giving a one-shoulder shrug. "Why?"

"I hate to be the one to tell you this, but you might want to stay away from that woman. There's rumor going around that she's on the warpath and going after anyone she thinks might be interested in her husband. I overheard her telling him you were off limits." Before I had a chance to pick my chin up off the floor, she continued. "I'm not saying I believe them, but if I were you, I wouldn't take any chances." She shook her head. "You never know about anyone when it comes to matters of the heart."

Chapter 8

It took me a while to find my voice, but after a few more deep breaths, I finally managed to speak. "Why would people think she's doing it?" I'd been taking so many deep breaths I worried about hyperventilating. So I relaxed my shoulders and closed my eyes momentarily. When I opened my eyes I caught Betty staring at me.

"Well …" Betty sat down on the edge of the bed and held up a hand. She touched her index finger. "First of all, it's not a secret that her husband is a womanizer. He was seen with both of the ladies who died a few months ago." She touched her next finger. "And everyone knows he and Aileen … well, they didn't do a very good job of hiding their relationship, if you know what I mean."

This was getting weirder by the hour. Here I was, minding my own business and trying to relax on a humongous cruise ship, when a small group of people found me and stuck me right smack dab in the middle of a murder scandal. Mama had always told me to be careful who I chose to hang out with. Her words, "They'll just drag you down to their level, and before you know it, you're as bad as they are," popped into my head. She was so right.

"Are you listening to me, Autumn?" Betty made a sour face. "You remind me of my granddaughter. She zones out when I tell her something she doesn't want to hear."

"No, I heard you."

Betty stood and wagged her finger in my face. "Stay away from Judith and Harvey, or you'll find yourself sucked down into a tube of trouble that you'll never be able to get out of."

Tube of trouble? That was the first time I'd ever heard that expression, and I thought it sounded like something Mama would have come up with. But I didn't say anything. I just nodded.

"Okay, then, I'd better get going. I don't want to miss bingo in the casino." She took a couple of steps toward the door. "Oh, sorry, where on earth are my manners? Would you like to join me?" She looked me up and down. "If you want to, you'll have to change into something a little nicer."

"I appreciate the offer, but no thank you. I'll stick around here tonight."

"Maybe you can play Bunko with a group of us tomorrow night. Judith will probably be there, but I'll make sure she doesn't bother you."

"Thanks." I saw her to the door, closed it after she left, and locked it behind her. This has been one of the strangest nights of my life, and my conversation with Betty was the oddest one of them all. I had no intention of playing Bunko or doing anything with her tomorrow night, but I didn't feel like telling her. Besides, if everything went the way I wanted it to, I'd be on a flight heading back to Nashville by then.

I waited a little while before calling the information desk to find someone to talk to about leaving the ship. It was a frustrating experience because no one of any authority was available to speak to me, unless it was an emergency. I decided to wait until first thing in the morning to try to chat with the captain.

When I booked my cruise, I had imagined myself having fun laughing with other passengers, playing charades on the Lido Deck, and doing the bunny hop around the ship. Instead, I was here, hovering in my room, scared for my life, and wishing I'd gone to Destin or Myrtle Beach instead.

As I sat there trying to figure out what to do with my time, I finally figured it would be worth whatever it cost in roaming charges to talk to Summer. She was the smartest person I knew, and she had experience with all kinds of people and situations I'd never been exposed to.

It took me a while to make the connection, but I finally got Summer on the line. "I can't believe you're actually calling me," she said. "You're supposed to be partying the night away. Aren't there any cute guys to hang out with?"

"I wouldn't know." Then I jumped right into what

had been happening since I'd been on the ship.

"Oh wow. Trouble sure did find you fast, didn't it?" Summer chuckled. "That's what always happens to me. Must run in the family."

"Yeah, so I'm planning to catch a flight home tomorrow after we reach the port."

"Come on, Autumn. Don't tell me you're going to wig out on finding out who did it."

"I'm not you."

"I know that, but we still share some of the same DNA. Aren't you the least bit curious?"

"Well ... yes."

"Then pay close attention, and you might wind up helping them solve this case."

"I wouldn't even know where to start," I admitted. "Remember I've never been in law enforcement, so the only thing I can actually see myself getting into is a bunch of trouble."

"Since I assume you're calling for advice, I'll be happy to give it to you."

She was right, but now I wondered what I'd been thinking deep down. Subconsciously, I was probably hoping she'd tell me to get off the ship as fast as I could.

For the next ten minutes, she asked questions and gave me a list of things to do. "However," she added, "if you leave the ship tomorrow, don't do any of that because it'll come back and bite you in the backside later. Just come on home. But trust me, if you're anything like me, it'll drive you crazy later."

"Why would it drive me crazy to get out of this

insanity that clearly isn't a safe place to be?"

"You'll wonder what happened, who did it, and if you could have helped solve the crime." She paused. "And maybe even save a life or two."

"Why did you have to put it that way?"

"Because it's true."

"I wish you were here," I admitted.

"Ya know, so do I. You really should have called me. I could have used a cruise."

"Would you have dropped everything and come with me?"

"Probably. I'm starting to think I should never have left law enforcement, and a cruise might have been just the thing to help clear my mind. The longer I'm away, the more I miss it."

"Mama says you're working temp jobs and loving it."

"Yes, I'm working temp jobs," she said. "But loving it? Not so much. Most of them bore me to tears."

We talked for a few more minutes, and she told me several things to do. I jotted everything on the back of an envelope I found in my handbag.

After I got off the phone, I knew my bill would be groaning with the roaming charges. It cost a fortune to make calls at sea, but I was still glad I did it.

Summer had told me that I needed to try to see the woman who was poisoned as soon as possible. It seemed dangerous to go to the infirmary, but she said that it wasn't any more dangerous than any place else on the ship since we had no idea who did it.

I had no reason to believe that Aileen had left the

infirmary, so I exited my cabin and made my way in that direction. When I spotted someone coming toward me, I tried to duck out of sight, but that quickly became impossible because the corridor was so narrow. If I kept that up, the other passengers would think I was doing something shady.

The infirmary was on the lower deck, and I had a pretty good idea where it was. Once I got in the general vicinity, I asked a couple of the other passengers, and they pointed the way.

To my surprise, Doc Healey was sitting there flipping through a magazine when I walked in. Since it didn't look like he heard me at first, I shuffled my feet and cleared my throat. He glanced up and smiled.

"What can I do for you?" He put down the magazine and stood, gesturing toward the seat to offer it to me. "Are you not feeling well, or are you hurt?"

"No, I'm feeling fine."

"Good." He flashed a genuine smile. "So what are you here for?"

"I-I came to see if Aileen Graves was still here." It seemed strange since I didn't know her, but I figured Summer would only give me good advice.

"Are you a friend of Ms. Graves?"

I shook my head. "No, but I wanted to stop by and visit her. I've heard that she's not doing well, and I thought she might be lonely."

Doc Healey frowned as he pondered what to do. He finally blew out a breath as he nodded. "I guess it's okay, but let me check with her first. What did you say your name is?"

"Autumn Spencer." I hoped that wouldn't get my name on some sort of suspect list, but it was too late now.

"Okay, stay here. I'll be right back."

He opened the door in the back of the waiting area, glanced over his shoulder at me as if making sure I didn't go anywhere, and then disappeared. I took a look at the magazine he'd been reading and saw that it was for golfers. It made me smile as I thought about the irony of a ship doctor not having an opportunity to play much golf since he was stuck onboard for weeklong cruises.

I looked around at the rest of the reception area. There were several posters similar to what I'd seen in my doctor's office—labeled images of the human body, warnings about the consequences of not being vaccinated, and tips on how to prevent heart disease. And there were other posters of exotic beaches designed to tempt passengers to book their next cruise.

When he came back, he held the door open. "She says she doesn't know who you are, but she'll talk to you for a few minutes. I think you were right about her being lonely."

I followed him to another room. The infirmary wasn't huge, but it was bigger than I'd expected.

As soon as I saw the woman half sitting up on the cot, my nerves got the best of me. I had no idea what to say, and her skin was so pale I could tell she hadn't fully recovered from whatever she'd ingested.

She frowned as she looked into my eyes. "Who are

you and what are you doing here?"

Chapter 9

Now that she'd asked me point blank, I couldn't answer her. It didn't seem right to ask her how she was feeling or if she knew what substance was used in her attempted murder since she didn't know me. So I cleared my throat a few times. "I thought you might be lonely."

She rolled her eyes. "Loneliness I can handle. Cyanide, I can't. So if you're here to finish killing me, go right ahead. It couldn't be any worse than what I've already been through."

"Are you sure it was cyanide? What else did you eat recently"

Her eyes narrowed to slits, and she tilted her head. "Are you a cop?"

"No, why?"

She waved her hand around. "The way you asked me, you sounded like you were here to question me."

I thought about that for a moment before gesturing toward the chair. Apparently, a few minutes on the phone with Summer had rubbed off on me. "Mind if I sit down?"

She made a face. "Go ahead, I can't stop you."

Her attitude didn't make me want to stay, but I was more curious than I was eager to leave. "Regardless of what it was, it's terrible."

"You don't have to tell me, young lady. Remember, I'm the one who ate the poison." She tilted her head and gave me a look from beneath her heavily made-up eyebrows. "I'm the one who got sick as a dog. It was poison."

"Do you have any idea who might have done that?"

"Oh, I'm sure plenty of people would like to get rid of me, but I don't know of anyone who'd be willing to spend time in jail for it." She contorted her mouth. "Of course, that means someone would have to be competent enough to catch the murderer, and that's not likely to happen around here."

Good point, but I didn't tell her that. "I hear you take a lot of cruises."

Her head snapped around. "Who told you that?"

Since I didn't want to mention anyone's name, I shrugged. "A lot of people here are worried about you, and I picked up on the fact that you're well known on the ship."

A hint of a smile played on her lips, surprising me but alerting me to the fact that she enjoyed attention. "Yes, I suppose I am rather famous on the sea."

I hadn't used the word *famous*, but I knew better than to correct her since she obviously liked the idea of being famous. "Where are you from?"

Again, suspicion clouded her eyes. "Why do you want to know?" Before I had a chance to answer, she added, "If you're not a cop, why would you care?"

"I don't like to hear about anyone being poisoned."

She smirked. "Especially since you're on the same ship, and you can't run away from someone trying to murder you."

I had a bunch more questions rattling around in my mind, but after her responses, I decided not to ask them. So I stood to leave.

"Where are you going?"

"I get the feeling you don't want me here."

She made another face, only this one was somewhat comical. "Why would you say that? I never told you I didn't want you here."

This woman was truly clueless about a lot of things, including her antagonistic behavior. "You don't have to tell me. It's obvious."

She flopped back on the cot. "Suit yourself. Everyone is always in a hurry to go somewhere, even when they don't know where they're going."

"True." I paused and pondered what to do. "You're right. I don't have anywhere to go, but I don't want to stick around if my being here makes you feel worse, and that's the impression I'm getting."

Aileen lifted an arm over her head and groaned. "I doubt it's possible to feel any worse than I've felt since I came to." Then she wrapped her arms around her midsection. "Whatever I ate gave me the worst stomach ache I've ever had in my life." She made a face. "Not only that, it made me dizzy, confused, and overall just not myself."

"Maybe you should rest, then."

"You really are in a hurry to leave, aren't you?"

Now I was. Her attitude was angering me, and it took a lot to make me mad. Besides, I reminded myself once again that I came on the cruise to rest and relax, not get into a verbal battle with a cranky woman who'd upset someone enough to try to murder her.

Without another word, I left her room and walked up toward the reception area where I spotted the doctor back in the chair, flipping pages in the magazine. He glanced up at me and started to stand.

"You don't have to get up. I'm leaving."

"You don't look happy." He grinned as he repositioned himself in the chair.

"She's a handful."

He made a face. "To put it mildly."

I looked around the room and then let my gaze meet his again. "Are you sure she ingested cyanide?"

"Pretty sure but not 100 percent."

"Why would anyone want to do away with her?"

He shrugged. "Why do people want to do anything? Usually murder involves jealousy or greed. Since she spent every extra penny on cruises, and as far as I can tell, she doesn't have much to spare, that leaves us with jealousy."

I pondered what he said for a moment before I nodded. "Interesting."

He shut the magazine and stood. "By the way, I

spoke to the captain while you were with Mrs. Graves. He wants us to keep mum about what happened to her."

"Is it hurting business that much?"

"Of course it is. But that's not why. The authorities have said that the less information we let out the easier it will be to catch whoever is poisoning people. Apparently, the deaths we had onboard in the past are now under investigation as well." He grimaced as soon as he said that. "I shouldn't have told you that."

"So it wasn't a supergerm?"

He gave me a closed-mouth smile as his eyes gave me the answer. Finally, he shook his head. "I didn't say that. All I'm saying is this needs to be kept under wraps."

"There are others who know about what happened," I countered.

"That's true, but they've already been spoken to."

I couldn't see how they could keep the information contained, now that some of the biggest mouths on the ship had enough information to run with it, but I wasn't in the position of arguing. "I won't say a word to anyone."

He nodded. "I never doubted you'd cooperate. You seem like an agreeable type."

That was part of my problem. I was too agreeable ... always. And that was one of the main reasons I needed to get away. As soon as someone said they needed me, I jumped. At school, when the principal couldn't find another teacher to serve on the PTA board, she turned to me. Of course I did it, just as she knew I would. When one of my family members got sick, I showed up at their door with a casserole. When the church needed someone to organize an event, they turned to me. When Mama or Daddy needed help with something, I didn't hesitate to come through.

"Is there anything I can do for you?" the doctor asked.

I realized I'd been standing in the same spot, staring at the wall. I shook my head. "No, but thanks. I need to leave so you can do your job."

He laughed as he held up the magazine. "As if I have all that much to do." His expression changed back to a more serious one. "Would you be interested in joining me for dinner tonight? Normally we frown on staff and passengers socializing, but I asked the captain, and he said it would be okay … that is, if you're interested."

For the first time I saw him as a man outside of being the ship's doctor. He wasn't the best looking guy I'd ever met, but he was somewhat pleasant looking. And I liked his demeanor—laid back and nice. No doubt he was smart, or he wouldn't have been able to become a doctor.

"If you're sure the captain doesn't mind, and you won't get in trouble—"

"I won't get in trouble."

We made plans to meet outside the infirmary at 6:00 PM because he needed to eat early. "You'll need to dress up, though." He gave me an apologetic look. "Staff is expected to—"

I interrupted him. "That's fine. I like dressing up."

"Good. See you tonight."

After I left, I went to my cabin to freshen up and to process all I'd discovered. As I turned the last corner on the way, I literally bumped into Jerome Pratt, the ship's purser. I had to place my hand on the wall to steady myself.

"Sorry." He blinked momentarily and then kept going, which I thought was odd. Most of the crewmembers were extremely polite, and his reaction bordered on rudeness.

I made my way to my room, still somewhat dazed by being jostled, when I heard my name being called from a couple of doors down. I glanced up and saw Betty motioning for me to get closer. In spite of the fact that I wasn't in the mood to talk to her, I did as she wanted.

"You haven't told anyone about Aileen, have you?"

"Haven't told anyone *what* about Aileen?" I lifted my fingers to my lips and made a zipping motion.

She rolled her eyes. "You know what I'm talking about."

Of course I did. "I haven't brought her up to anyone, if that's what you're talking about."

"No one needs to know she survived." She tipped her head forward and gave me one of her annoying warning looks. "Everyone but just a few of us think she died."

That wasn't what I expected. "Why would everyone think that?"

"Because that's what happens when people eat

poison."

I hated being talked to like I was a child. "I know that, but I don't think anyone is supposed to know she was poisoned."

"Oh, trust me, a lot of folks on the ship knows someone was poisoned. A bunch of them have been asking for a refund."

"How do you know this?"

She bobbed her head. "I have ways of finding out stuff … and I have ears."

"Whatever the case, I'm not planning to tell anyone anything. It's not mine to tell."

"So how do you like Doc Healey?" She folded her arms and gave me a sly smile. "He's quite a catch, don't you think?"

"Catch?"

"Yes, don't you have a date with him tonight?"

Chapter 10

Now I was nervous. How on earth could Betty possibly know I was having dinner with the doctor, unless she was right there with us? Or unless the doctor had called and told her. That pretty much creeped me out.

I took a step back. "I wouldn't call it a date. We're just having dinner."

"Call it what you want, Autumn, but in my day, when a woman had dinner with a man, it was called a date."

I wasn't sure what to say about having dinner with Doc Healey, so I changed the subject. "How are you feeling?"

Betty scrunched her nose. "It's none of your business how I'm feeling. Why would you ask such a silly question?"

"I'm …" There was no point in explaining or apologizing, so I let my voice trail off. "I'd better go. If you don't need anything …"

"I do need something."

Dread washed over me as I tried to imagine what this woman could possibly want from me. And it made me feel guilty that I had no desire to do whatever it was she was about to ask me to do.

"Can you run to the store and pick up a few things for me?"

"Now?"

"Yes, now." She placed a hand on her hip and bobbed her head. "You don't think I would have summoned you if I didn't want you to do it now, do you?" She pulled her head back and gave me a long look. "Don't tell me you thought I just wanted to chat."

Was she completely unaware of how rude she was being? What was up with these bossy passengers?

She pulled a slip of paper from her pocket and handed it to me. "Here's my list. Just tell them to put it on my account."

I glanced at it and saw a list of various types of candy bars, a digestive aid, and a bottle of pain relievers. "Can it wait just a little while? I can let you borrow some of my Advil if you have a headache."

"No, I want that stuff now ... or at least as quickly as you can get it for me."

The tone of her voice sounded desperate, and I wasn't in the mood to argue or even talk with her any longer than I had to. Running down to the ship's store would at least get me away for a little while. So I finally nodded. "Okay, I'll go get it now."

"Good girl. Hurry."

Instead of heading back to my cabin first, I made

an about-face and went straight toward the store. I couldn't find a couple of the candy bars, so I went to the clerk and asked about them.

"You wouldn't, by any chance, be picking up these items for Betty Farber, would you?"

I hadn't yet told her to charge the purchase to Betty's account, and that made me wonder how she knew. "I am. Why?"

She closed her eyes and shook her head. "She does this on every single cruise."

"Does what?"

"She picks someone—typically a young woman traveling alone—and has them run errands for her." The clerk put the items in a bag. "And she always asks for the same candy bars, even though she knows we don't carry all of them. I don't know why she keeps doing the same thing but expecting something different." A grin formed on the clerk's face. "And you realize that's the definition of insanity, right?"

"Maybe she's hoping you'll get them in if she keeps asking."

"Maybe, or—" She pressed her lips together.

"Maybe what?"

"Never mind. Is there anything else you need while you're here? We have a special on sun visors and sunscreen."

"No, that's okay, but thanks. I really need to get moving."

"If you don't want to keep running down here, remind Ms. Farber that we deliver."

"I'm surprised she doesn't already know that."

"Oh, she does." The clerk smiled again. "But for some reason she seems to enjoy having other passengers do this for her."

I felt my shoulders sag as I gave in to my thoughts and feelings. "That's rather strange, don't you think?"

"It is, but if you know Betty …" She shrugged. "She's different. After a while, you come to expect odd behavior. Just be careful, and if you can do it without being obvious, you might want to avoid her."

"Really? I don't want to be mean to her."

"I'm not saying you have to be mean, but there is usually more than one way to go where you need to be."

I smiled at the woman who I suspected was on the same page as me. But that still didn't negate the fact that I wasn't getting what I needed out of this cruise.

When I arrived at Betty's cabin door, she flung it open before I had a chance to knock. "Did you get everything on my list?"

"Unfortunately, no. They didn't have some of the candy bars you wanted."

She scowled as she grabbed the bag from me, opened it, and glanced inside. "And why didn't they?"

"I have no idea. The clerk said—"

"I don't know why on earth they don't carry stuff people keep asking for." She turned around and tossed the sack onto the dresser before facing me again. "Want to come in? I have some of my homemade cherry brandy. I don't drink it myself, but people tell me it's good. Harvey Bailey can't seem to get enough, so I usually make a couple of bottles just for him. The captain likes it too. And my late husband, rest his soul—"

"I appreciate the offer, but no, I really need to start getting ready."

She looked me up and down. "What's wrong with the way you look now?"

"I don't think anything's wrong with how I look, but I need to freshen my makeup and put on something a little dressier."

"Oh, so now you care how you're dressed?" Betty shook her head. "You didn't seem to be concerned when I told you to put on something a little nicer."

"But I—"

"Oh, never mind. Go do whatever it is you have to do. Never mind that this little old lady ..." She tilted her head and gave me a pitiful look. "This *lonely* little old lady has something to say."

She sure did know how to pull my strings. "I can stick around for a few minutes."

"No, you said it yourself. You need to get ready."

"I'm sorry. It's just that ..." My voice trailed off as I realized I didn't have anything else to add.

She leaned forward and placed her hand on my arm. "Seriously, Autumn, you might want to consider staying closer to home for your next vacation. I don't think you're cut out for cruising."

I was sure that made sense to her, but she obviously didn't know anything about me. Besides, who was she to talk since she spent all her time on the ship? "How about you, Betty? Why do you cruise?"

She shrugged. "Got nothing better to do."

"Do you have a home?" I cleared my throat. "I mean on land?"

"What business is that of yours?"

"Sorry." I lowered my gaze. She was right. It was absolutely none of my business.

"Don't get all worked up, Autumn. You're way too sensitive for your own good." She paused. "If it makes you feel any better, yes, I do have a house on land."

"That's nice."

"No, it's terrible. My children—my grown children—have already started fighting over who gets it when I'm gone. That's why I hate going home. They stick me right in the middle of their stupid squabbles. I kept hoping they'd grow up and move far away, but every stinkin' one of them bought a house within a mile from where they grew up. Why couldn't they be like most kids?" I thought she was finished until she opened her mouth and continued her rant. "That's not all. When I'm home, they expect me to drop everything and babysit when they want to go out."

Now I had way more information than I asked for or even wanted, so I took a step back, hoping to get away before this conversation got any more personal. But she reached out and yanked me back before I could make a break for it.

"But I've got news for them. I've already set up my will, and not a one of them will get the house or anything of value."

"I'm sure everything will work out."

She cackled. "I just wish I could be there for the reading of my will. I tried to talk my attorney into staging my death so I could see the looks on their faces when they find out the only thing they'll be left with is each other ..." She lifted her hands. "And then I'd pop out of the closet and shock them."

This conversation was getting on my nerves. "Betty, I really need to go now."

"Suit yourself. I don't know why I thought you'd be any different from the others."

"The others?"

"Yeah, all the other young people who try to get favors from me. They make nice with me, but when I ask for one thing, they want to turn and run." She made an exaggerated sigh. "I suppose that's how kids are today. There's no telling what'll happen to society after my generation is gone."

As tempting as it was to defend myself—and my generation—I resisted the urge. All she was doing was getting me worked up over something that didn't really matter in my life and had absolutely nothing to do with me. Based on the look on her face, I was pretty sure she knew what she was doing, and I could tell she enjoyed every minute of it too.

I finally managed to get away from her and into my cabin. After closing the door, I locked it and threw myself across the bed. If I'd known earlier in the year what I knew now, I either would have booked my vacation somewhere in the mountains or at the beach. But it was too late for that, so I planned to make the most of what I had.

I was excited about wearing one of the gowns I'd purchased when Dillard's had their end-of-season sale.

It had a black background, an empire waistline, and teal sparkles on the bodice.

I stood in front of the full-length mirror and did my slightly wavy hair in the up-do I'd been practicing for weeks. Then I topped off my makeup and added some coral lipstick for that extra pop of color. I hoped I was dressed appropriately for dinner with Doc Healey.

Since I didn't feel like running into Betty again, I quietly slipped out of my cabin and went in the other direction. Even though it was a longer route to the infirmary, I wasn't in the mood for another lecture.

I was about to make my last turn toward where I was supposed to meet Doc Healey when I heard a couple of people talking. I slowed down right before I recognized Harvey Bailey's voice. "Do you think Autumn knows about Charlie?"

"Oh, I'm sure she doesn't," Judith replied. "Because if she did, she'd never agree to have dinner with him. From what I've seen, she's not one to take risks like that."

"Yeah, she does seem a bit stodgy for someone her age."

"Not only that, she doesn't seem to know much about human nature, let alone the signs of a man who's desperate."

I stopped in my tracks and caught my breath. What had I gotten myself into?

Harvey belted out a laugh. "I'm sure she'll find out, though. That's not an easy secret to keep, and he's never been good with a poker face."

Chapter 11

Okay, now I was confused. I wasn't sure whether I should continue on as though I hadn't heard anything or if I should go to my cabin, lock the door, and not come back out until I could leave the ship … or something else.

I leaned against the wall, chewed on my bottom lip as I took a couple of breaths, and tried to make some sense of their conversation. But it was impossible, considering the fact that I didn't have a clue what they were talking about. My next thought was *What would Summer do?*

They changed the subject, as their voices grew faint, indicating they were heading in the other direction. I let out a breath, squared my shoulders, and lifted my chin. I needed to follow through with my plans since I'd committed, but I now knew I needed to watch for signs of some secret that I needed to know.

Unfortunately, Harvey and Judith were probably right about the fact that I didn't understand human nature. I'd been fooled and hurt by people so many times throughout my life I'd sworn off dating for a while or getting close to new people I met. For some reason, I thought having dinner with Doc Healey would be harmless, but apparently, even that could be dangerous.

After I thought the Baileys were no longer in the corridor, I peeked around the corner to make sure. Good. They were gone.

In spite of what they'd said, I was disappointed that Doc Healey wasn't in front of the infirmary waiting for me. Maybe he said he'd be inside. I saw that the OPEN sign hung on the door.

So I grabbed the knob and slowly turned it. As I pushed it open, I gasped. Doc Healey was nowhere in sight, but there was a woman sprawled out on the floor, clearly unconscious.

I leaned over, lifted her arm, and checked her pulse. She barely had one, so I rushed out into the hallway and hollered for help.

The first person who appeared was a man on his way to the dining room. He was dressed in a tux, so I didn't expect him to come running, but he did. He checked the woman's pulse and agreed with me—that she needed immediate medical care.

"Where's the ship's doctor?" he asked.

"I have no idea. I was supposed to meet him here five minutes ago."

He took a step back, looked me up and down, and slowly shook his head. "Looks to me like the two of you won't be going anywhere—that is, if he ever shows up."

The sound of more footsteps coming toward us grabbed our attention. The first person to walk in was the captain, looking frazzled and annoyed. He narrowed his eyes and glared at me. "Where's Doc Healey?"

"We were supposed to—"

"What's going on here?"

The sound of Doc Healey's voice gave me a momentary surge of relief, until he knelt down, felt the woman's pulse, and shook his head. "It doesn't look good."

He looked past me and started barking orders at someone behind me. I turned around and saw Andrea standing by the door, her face scrunched in concern. She nodded and left.

Doc and a couple of the men lifted her to a gurney, and he sprang into action with needles and tubes. I had to look the other way, but I didn't want to leave.

There was so much commotion I figured I was in the way where I stood. So I took a few steps back until Doc Healey managed to eventually get the woman stabilized.

"It's easy to treat someone when you know what happened."

I glanced over my shoulder at the deep masculine voice. I'd seen this man on the ship, but I had no idea who he was.

He shook his head, as he looked me in the eyes. "Everyone knows the doctor on this ship is bored, so he does things to liven it up a bit."

"What are you talking about?" I tilted my head but managed to hold his gaze.

He pulled me off to the side. "I've been watching the crew, and something seems mighty fishy with a couple of them—mostly the doctor."

"Really?" Goosebumps ran down my spine and arms. "You think he's guilty of something?"

"I can't say that I know anything for sure, but look at him." He gestured toward the doctor. "He appears to be enjoying himself a tad more than he should."

I looked at Doc Healey and saw what the man was talking about. But I didn't want to think he might do something unethical ... or illegal.

"You don't think he ..." I grimaced. "I mean, you're not saying he ..." I couldn't get the words out.

"Are you trying to ask if I think he might have murdered those people?"

That was exactly what I was thinking but didn't want to say. Not only did I not know this man, I wasn't sure what he knew. "I'm not sure what I'm trying to ask."

He gave me a half smile. "Let me just put it this way. I wanted to leave the ship, but my wife insisted we stay until the end. After this experience, I won't go with this cruise line ever again."

I doubted I'd ever cruise on *any* ship again, but I didn't say that. Instead, I simply nodded.

"My wife asked me to come down here and see what all the hullabaloo was about. After I tell her, she might finally agree with me."

I smiled. "I was supposed to have dinner with the doctor, but it looks like that won't be happening … at least not tonight."

He gave me a stern but caring look. "You and I obviously don't know each other, but you look to be close to my daughter's age, so I'm going to give you the same advice I'd give her." He paused, as his look grew even more serious. "Don't get involved with any of the crew on this ship, or any other cruise line for that matter. They have a job to do, and nothing good will ever come of a relationship with any of them."

"I appreciate your advice." And I did, although I probably wouldn't have listened to him if he'd said the same thing a few hours ago.

"Hey, I have an idea. Why don't you join the wife and me for dinner, since your date is obviously occupied with something else?"

"I don't want to impose."

"You won't be imposing. We signed up to be at a big table to meet other people, but since this ship is no longer full, we have plenty of room."

"Are you sure?" I asked.

"You must be from the South."

I nodded. "Did my accent give me away?"

"Well …" He grinned. "That and the fact that you're so concerned about not imposing. The only other person I ever knew who did that was my mother who was from Mississippi."

"I'm from Nashville."

"There ya go. That explains it." He gestured toward the hallway. "Let's go get my wife and head on

82

over to the dining room."

We were a few feet away from his cabin when the door opened and a beautiful woman about the age of my mother walked out. She smiled at her husband and then looked at me. "Bringing home strays again, George?"

The twinkle in her eyes let me know this was some sort of private joke between them. He laughed.

"She had a date with the ship's doctor, who is tending to the commotion we heard earlier."

The woman lifted her hands. "Say no more." She leaned toward me and cupped her hands for a whisper. "My husband doesn't trust this ship's crew."

I nodded. "Yes, he told me that."

"By the way, my name is Maria." She extended her hand, and I took it. Then she pulled me in for a hug. "You remind me of our daughter."

"That's what I told her." He glanced at me again. "In case you haven't figured it out yet, I'm George … George Pickard."

"It's nice to meet y'all. Should I call you Mr. and Mrs. Pickard?"

"No way." George shook his head. "You're an adult. Call us by our first names."

Maria nudged her husband. "She might look like our daughter, but she sounds like your mother."

"God rest her soul." George held out his hand toward the direction we were heading. "Let's get going. I don't want to be late for dinner."

"My husband hates being late for any meal," Maria teased.

"Hey." George feigned a hurt look. "Eating is my favorite hobby."

Maria linked arms with me. "I'm afraid it's become his *only* hobby. We'll need to get him on the dance floor after dinner to work off some of it." She paused. "You are planning to go stay for the party after dinner, aren't you?"

Chapter 12

I actually had no idea what I was going to do next, let alone what I wanted to do after dinner. My nature was to dart back to my room and stay there until the next morning, but I knew I needed to get out more, and I was pretty sure I wasn't any safer in my cabin than I would be out in the public. So I nodded. "I will, at least for a little while."

Maria beamed. "Good. It's time for you to have some fun."

When we arrived in the dining room, the hostess greeted us. George explained that I was switching my seating arrangement, and she accepted that without argument. I followed them to the table.

We had a lovely dinner, and like George had said, the table wasn't full. In fact, the dining room appeared to be half empty.

"This is strange," Maria said as we nibbled on our dessert. "Every other cruise we've gone on has been booked full."

"That's because we booked cruises with companies that took care of their passengers, not killed them."

"I'm sure it was all accidental, George. No one killed anyone … at least not on purpose." Maria flipped her hand from the wrist as she turned to me. "He gets so worked up about nothing."

George widened his eyes. "People died on this boat, Maria." He glanced at me with a solemn expression before turning back to his wife. "And now they're getting sick. I wouldn't say that's nothing."

"That's not what I'm saying." Maria propped her elbows on the table and leaned toward her husband. "We're here, so we need to make the most of it." She turned to me. "I knew he was scared when he said he didn't want to eat the food, but I finally convinced him that everything's been cleaned up, and all the germs have been demolished."

"At first we believed them when they said they had some supergerm that needed to be cleaned up." George held up his index finger. "But I'm thinking it wasn't germs that killed those people. The woman in the clinic looked like she might have been poisoned."

I wondered if they knew about Aileen, but I didn't mention her because I'd given my word, plus I figured that would only make matters worse. We were captive on the ship—at least until we docked—so there was no point in causing more panic than there already was.

For the first time since I'd boarded the ship, I truly had a good time. These people, George and Maria, seemed more normal than the other folks I'd met.

They were more like me, and they didn't seem like the type to create drama just for the sake of entertainment. And as strange as it might have sounded, it even comforted me that George had the same concerns I had.

The party after dinner featured a variety of music—from hip-hop to polka—and we danced to all of it. George started a conga line, and by the end of the song, everyone was up and dancing. I couldn't remember ever laughing so hard as when some of the elderly ladies my grandmother's age let loose and showed that folks were never too old to kick up their heels.

I'd never been one to stay out late, so I was tired long before I knew the party would end. And I didn't want to leave because I was afraid I'd miss out.

We were about to start karaoke when Maria leaned over and whispered, "Don't look now, but your friend the doctor has just entered the room."

I glanced up and saw Doc Healey looking around the ballroom, until he finally spotted me. He smiled and started walking straight toward us. George groaned. "I could have done without him tonight."

I agreed, but once again, I didn't want to be rude. So I greeted him when he approached. The first thing he did was talk to George. "Thank you for taking care of my date."

This annoyed me because I didn't feel that I had to be taken care of. George saw my annoyance and chuckled. Then he pulled Maria to her feet and led her to stand in line for singing.

Once I was alone with the doctor, I wasn't sure what to say. I shifted my weight from one foot to the other and looked around before smiling at him. "How's that woman in the clinic?"

"She's doing much better. In fact, she regained consciousness shortly after we administered the IV."

"That's a relief."

Doc Healey smiled and took my hand. "Having fun?"

"Yes, I am."

"Good. Can I get you something to drink?"

I let go of him and put my hands around the glass of ginger ale. "I'm fine."

The server approached and asked him what he wanted. "I'll have what she's having."

The server's eyebrows shot up and a look of amusement played on her lips. "Okie dokey."

When she came back with his drink, he lifted it and took a long swig. Then he crinkled his nose. "What is this stuff?"

"Ginger ale."

"But there's nothing good in it."

"It's straight ginger ale," I said. "That's all I wanted."

"How can you drink it?" He lifted his index finger to summon the server. "I can't drink this stuff straight. Bring me a bourbon."

"Coming right up."

After the server left, he turned to me. "Yeah, we managed to get our sick passenger up and talking. It was touch-and-go for a while, but I managed to bring her to."

"What happened?"

"Apparently she ate at the buffet but ingested something different from what the others had."

"What others are you talking about?"

"Her friends." He looked away from me for a moment.

"Any idea what it was?"

"Not yet." The doctor accepted the drink the server brought, placed it on the table, and stared at it for a few seconds before lifting his gaze to mine. "I wish we could figure out what's happening. I thought we'd gotten past the worst of it, and then Aileen ... and now"

I leveled him with a long gaze. "What do you think is happening, Doc Healey?"

He shook his head and dropped the smile momentarily. I got the impression that this was taking its toll on him, but I still couldn't tell whether or not it was an act. "I sure wish I knew. Unfortunately, I'm getting some of the blame for not keeping everyone well." He cleared his throat. "And by the way, please call me Charlie."

"Okay ... Charlie." It seemed weird calling him by his first name. "I wonder why you're getting blamed."

The sides of his lips tilted into a smile as he shrugged. "It just comes with the territory."

"What brought you to work for the cruise line?" I asked.

"After my residency, I started to join my father's practice, but I knew I'd never be able to measure up to him. After saving so many lives, he was a hero in our town. One of my friends from medical school had started working on a cruise ship, and he had all these stories about traveling all over the world and getting paid to do it."

"I can see how that would appeal to a young doctor."

He grimaced. "It's not nearly as glamorous as he made it out to be. What he didn't tell me was that the ship's doctor rarely gets to see the sights when we dock. There's so much paperwork and stuff to follow up on here … plus as long as some of the passengers stay onboard, someone has to be on the ship."

"Does that someone have to be a doctor?"

He shook his head. "Not necessarily, but the captain gets to decide who stays and who can leave …" He held out his hand and splayed his fingers. "I'm clearly not his favorite person here."

"Isn't there something you can do? Someone you can talk to?"

Again, he shook his head. "Nope. The captain is in charge here, and he never lets anyone forget."

That didn't sound right, but I didn't want to argue. "So where is that woman who got sick?"

"She's still in the infirmary. I had a talk with her, and unlike Aileen, she wants to leave the ship as soon as we dock."

"I wonder why Aileen doesn't."

"That's another question I have. She and the captain—" He clamped his mouth shut as soon as those words escaped.

"She and the captain what?"

"Never mind." He pulled his lips between his teeth and squeezed his eyes shut. "There are some things I wish I'd never seen."

Now my curiosity was higher than ever, but I didn't want to continue harping on Charlie. "Who's in the infirmary with her now?"

"I managed to talk the nurse into staying with her for a few hours so I could get away."

"I have to admit I can't fathom the level of stress you have to deal with." I tried to smile, but I knew it didn't come across genuine, so I relaxed my face. "Have you considered doing something else ... like working in a hospital or joining your dad?"

"My dad doesn't want me working with him anymore since he says I sold out, but I might eventually see if I can get on at a hospital as an emergency room doctor."

That sounded even more stressful to me, but again, I didn't want to express my thoughts. I heard some familiar voices come over the speakers, so I glanced up and saw my new friends on the stage, singing a love ballad. My heart melted as they looked into each other's eyes and sang words of everlasting devotion.

Charlie glanced up at the stage and then turned back to me. "You seem rather fond of the Pickards."

"They're such a nice couple."

"Be careful, Autumn. They've been on this ship before, and they're known for causing trouble."

Now alarm bells rang in my head. "They didn't tell

me that."

"Of course they didn't. And if you ask them, don't expect them to tell you otherwise. The last captain we had got them banned, but Captain Myers had it lifted."

"Does he know them?"

"That's what the crew is thinking ... but none of us can figure out why he'd do that, unless ..." He contorted his mouth as he reached for my hand. "I'm so sorry you're having to see all this on your vacation. This should be a relaxing time for you, but it seems to be the opposite."

I wanted to tell him that was fine, but it wasn't. So I just smiled at him and lowered my gaze.

"Too bad you chose a boat that has more than its share of issues."

Out of the corner of my eyes, I spotted the cruise director coming toward us, looking like she was on a mission. She stopped at the table. "Doc, I'm sorry to bother you now, but there's an emergency in the infirmary."

Chapter 13

Charlie hesitated less than a minute, but the instant I gave him a nod, he was gone. And I was relieved. He seemed nice enough, but I didn't want anything to do with whatever was happening, and being around him would make that impossible.

George and Maria sang a couple more songs before they finally came back to the table, breathless but happy. Maria reminded me of Rue McClanahan from "The Golden Girls" as she regaled her experience on stage.

"That's the most fun I've had in ages." Her smile and flushed cheeks warmed my heart. She clearly loved being in the spotlight, and her husband was happy to make that happen. I couldn't see any of what Charlie was talking about. They didn't seem at all like the troublemaking type.

"Isn't my girl a great singer?" George said, his eyes twinkling with pride.

"She is." What I didn't say was that he carried the

tune, and she basically followed. I thought it was sweet that he was giving her all the credit.

"Where did the doctor go?" Maria looked around the room and then back at me. "The two of you appeared to be getting along just fine."

"Yes, we get along great, but there's been an emergency in the infirmary."

Maria cast a quick glance in George's direction. "There always seems to be an emergency on this ship. I can't wait to leave."

That didn't appear to me to be the case. She and George still glowed from their stage time, and I knew they planned to stick around until the party was over and the last person left. But I didn't mention that.

"What's the matter, Autumn?" Maria tilted her head and gave me a motherly look.

"Nothing."

"You keep yawning."

George laughed. "She's probably bored to tears hanging out with us old people. I'm sure she's used to a lot more excitement than we'll ever have."

"No," I said. "Trust me, this is more exciting than what I'm used to. I'm just tired."

"Then go back to your cabin and get some rest." Maria gestured around the room. "Looks like you're not the only one. There's hardly anyone left."

"I think that's what I'll do. Have fun."

Both of them reached for a hug. When I got to Maria, she whispered, "Don't answer your door if anyone knocks. George is right. There's something going on here, and I don't want you to get hurt."

I nodded and then left. It was weird how her words and actions didn't jive. It was almost as though she knew something.

As I walked toward my room, I jumped at every shadow and sound. It was a relief to finally get to my cabin and close the door behind me. Once I locked myself in, I looked in the closet, pulled back the shower curtain and checked out the bathtub, and got down on the floor to check under the bed. This was all stuff I never would have done before, but I was getting paranoid. I pulled a chair over to the door and wedged it beneath the doorknob. If someone really wanted in, nothing would stop them, but I had to do something.

We were supposed to dock in St. Thomas the next day. I'd wanted to go on a walking tour, but now my plan was to find a way to leave. I knew it would be expensive if there were any seats left on the few flights out of there, but that was okay. I figured I could have a yard sale and sell a few things on eBay to replenish my bank account.

After I lay in bed for more than an hour with all kinds of thoughts rattling around in my head, I finally decided to talk to my cousin Summer again. It was late, but I was pretty sure she'd still be awake.

She answered right away. "I bet this is costing you a fortune," she said. "What's up? Have you found out what's going on with the murders?"

"I'm still not sure we're dealing with murders. No one has died during this cruise, but it looks like they've come awfully close." Then I told her all about the people I'd met and all the things that happened since we last spoke, including what Maria whispered.

"First of all, I'd try to find out what's going on with Maria and George. They sound like people of interest."

"Really? They seem so normal." The doctor's comments flashed through my head.

"Really. Some people are great actors. And keep your eyes and ears open for any interaction between the captain and the doctor. Something doesn't sound right there."

"Okay." I'd been thinking the exact same thing.

"And whatever you do, don't let yourself be alone with the doctor, and for heaven's sake, don't take a drink from him … or anyone else."

"You don't think—"

"Unless there's something you haven't told me, there's no way of knowing. All I'm saying is don't take a chance with anyone—particularly the crewmembers and repeat passengers."

I told her a little more about the other people on the ship. She seemed to think they were all suspects, even the purser, captain, and cruise director.

"There are so many different reasons someone would want to commit murder, you simply can't rule anyone out, at least not at this point."

"But I'm not a detective."

"Sorry, Autumn, but I disagree. If you're in the midst of a bunch of people being murdered, you have to have the discernment of a detective, just for self-protection."

"Okay, I get it." But deep down, I didn't get it. "Do you think I should abandon this cruise and fly home, after all that?"

"If you're really that afraid, yes." She paused. "But you're probably safe as long as you don't talk to too many people."

"What would you do if you were me?"

"I'd stick around and find out what's going on." She let out a nervous laugh. "But you're not me, which is a good thing. Don't forget that I get myself into the middle of all kinds of trouble."

"I've always looked up to you," I said.

Again, she laughed. "Don't. There's no doubt your parents are happy you didn't inherit some of my traits."

When silence fell between us, I remembered the cost of roaming charges on my phone. "I guess I'd better go. It's getting late."

"Call again if you need me."

After we hung up, I got ready for bed and crawled beneath the covers. I was still a little nervous about going to sleep, but since there was nothing I could do now, I forced myself to close my eyes. My mind swirled around for a few more minutes, but my sleepiness finally overcame my fear.

I awoke to the sound of more commotion out in the hallway. I got up, tiptoed to the door, and opened it a crack. I couldn't see anything or anyone, and the noise had diminished again. When would the craziness end?

This time it took me a half hour to get ready for the day. Once I was dressed and had on my bare-look makeup, I slowly opened the door and peeked out.

Whew! There was still nothing out there. Whatever I'd heard was obviously resolved.

My stomach made a hissing sound, reminding me that I needed to eat something. So I went to one of the smaller cafes and ordered some toast and coffee. "Are you sure that's all you want?" The server pointed to the buffet. "We have all kinds of fruit and eggs cooked almost any way you could possibly want them."

"Toast is fine for now."

She brought my order a few minutes later, so I sat there staring out the window at the deck as I nibbled on the toast. I spotted Betty walking by, so I quickly turned away, hoping she wouldn't see me. But it was too late. She wiggled her fingers, frowned, and then walked inside.

"You look horrible, Autumn." She placed her hand on my shoulder. "You're so tense. Why don't you join me at the spa?"

"I'm fine."

"You're clearly not getting the rest you need, and that's understandable considering how insane this place is." She paused. "Tell you what. If you come with me, I'll treat you to the works—massage, manicure, and hair."

"I can't—"

"You can, and you will." She leveled me with one of her firm motherly looks as she sat down across from me. "I'll wait until you finish eating." She narrowed her eyes as she saw what was in front of me. "Just toast and coffee? No wonder you look so gaunt. You need some protein and fruit. I'll go get you some."

Before I had a chance to argue, she got up and headed out toward the buffet. Apparently, I didn't have a choice in the matter, so I sank back and accepted the fact that I was being hovered over and cared for to the point of being pushed around. She walked back into the café with a satisfied expression on her face.

Fortunately, she didn't put too much on the plate—just a small scoop of scrambled eggs and a couple pieces of pineapple. "I didn't want to overwhelm you, but you have got to start eating nutritious food, or you're going to wind up sick."

My thoughts went back to the candy bars she'd asked me to pick up, but I didn't mention it. There wasn't any point in getting her worked up.

She glanced at her watch. "Hurry up, Autumn, or they won't be able to work you in. It'll get crowded in the spa in about an hour."

That would have suited me just fine, but I decided to go along with her since it appeared to be the path of least resistance. After I finished eating, I followed her to the spa, where she whispered something to the lady at the desk. The woman nodded, glanced over at me, and smiled. "We'll fix you right up. When you leave here, you'll be more relaxed than you've ever been."

A half hour later, I was lying face down on a table while some woman was kneading my back. I had to admit it felt good having the knots worked out. After the massage therapist finished with my back, she told me to get up and put on the robe she offered. I followed her to another small room, where Betty sat waiting for me.

"How was it?" she asked.

"Very nice."

"I thought you'd like it. Now it's time for the skin detox."

Within minutes, I was lying on my back and another woman wearing all white was slathering a pale green substance all over my body. After she finished, she told me to close my eyes so she could put some cucumbers on them.

I hated being in such a vulnerable position, but I did as I was told. Maybe this would help me relax.

After less than five minutes, I heard someone talking on the other side of a partition. The voice sounded familiar.

"Did you write the report yet?" a woman asked.

"I was just about to, but then I got violently sick."

"Yeah, the same thing happened to me. One minute I was writing my report and sipping on some cherry brandy, and next thing I know I'm in the infirmary."

"That's terrible, Aileen. Do you think they're on to us?"

Chapter 14

It took all of the self-restraint I could summon to stay in a prone position. I wanted to hop up and ask the women what they were talking about, but I knew that wouldn't serve any purpose other than to satisfy my curiosity.

"When I signed up to do mystery shopping on cruise ships, I didn't realize it involved risking my life."

"Yeah, me too. I thought it was an easy way to get a free cruise."

"It's been anything but easy. I've never been so sick in all my life."

"Do you think you might have eaten something?"

"Maybe. There's no telling on this ship. I don't think I'll ever do another mystery shop on a cruise."

"How about the captain?"

"That's been over for a long time."

They only said a few more things before one of them finally said, "We'd better be quiet. No telling who's listening. There seem to be a lot of nosy people around here."

"Yeah, I know. I can't wait to get off this stupid boat and go home. I'll stick to doing local restaurant mystery shops in the future."

"I like the ones for department stores. I've gotten some great loot from those."

A few minutes later, the woman who'd done my treatment returned. I heard her footsteps as soon as she entered my partitioned-off area, and I smelled her perfume when she got closer.

She lifted the cucumbers from my eyes and smiled down at me. "How ya feeling?"

I sighed. "Much better."

"You were rather peaked when you came in. Cucumber is good for getting rid of the bags, and you had enough to pack for a week's vacation." She let out a chuckle at her lame excuse for a joke. "Let's get you cleaned up so you don't look like a lagoon creature." She helped me sit up and led me to the shower.

After I rinsed off all the goop, I applied some moisturizer the woman handed me and then got dressed. Betty was waiting for me in the hair and nail salon.

She gave me a thumbs-up. "Lookin' good, Autumn. That's what a little bit of pampering will do for you."

I really did feel quite a bit better. My skin tingled, and my muscles were the most relaxed they'd been in a while. "Thank you so much for this."

"It's the least I could do after you dropped everything and ran that errand for me." She frowned momentarily and leaned toward me. "I overheard something that I need to tell you about." She nervously glanced around and lowered her voice to where I could barely hear her. "I think I know what's going on around here."

"Can we talk about it later?"

"Sure. Let's get our hair and nails done, and we can go to my cabin where there aren't so many nosy ears."

I had to bite the insides of my cheeks at her choice of words. As the hairdresser washed and blew my hair dry, I thought about everything and how it might all fit together. There were still quite a few gaping holes in the puzzle, but I was starting to fit a few of the more obvious pieces together.

"What color do you want?" Betty asked.

"Huh?"

"Nail polish. Do you want red, pink, orange …" She wiggled her eyebrows. "Or do you want to get wild with me and go for blue?"

I laughed. "If you can get wild, so can I."

She helped me pick a pretty robin's egg blue shade that was anything but wild, and the nail technician convinced me that some glitter on the tips would be like icing on the cake. When Betty saw that, she had some added to hers.

On the way back to her cabin, she chattered nonstop. "I feel so pretty now. Don't you feel pretty?" Before I had a chance to answer, she continued. "Too bad we're not looking for men. Well, maybe you are, but I'm not. At my age, they're more trouble than they're worth. They have to soak their teeth overnight, they get up once or twice … or more in the middle of the night." She shook her head. "I used to get so annoyed when the flushing toilet woke me up. I've always been a light sleeper."

When she finally stopped to catch a breath, I spoke up. "I don't think I'd want to look for a man on a cruise."

She gave me a funny look. "And why not?"

I shrugged. "I don't want to leave Nashville, and what are the chances I'd meet someone from there?"

"You could meet someone and have a fling. After the cruise, you can go your separate ways if you want to." She gave me a sly smile. "Not saying I've ever done that, but some people do."

"I'm not exactly the fling type."

She nodded. "Yeah, I can tell. You want to know what's wrong with you, Autumn?"

I didn't, but I knew she was going to tell me, whether I wanted her to or not. "What?"

"You're too serious. Everything seems to be black-and-white in your world."

My friends in high school and college had always told me that too, but I liked the way I was. It was time to get the conversation off of me and on to her. "How about you, Betty? Are you not a serious person?"

"Do you think I'd be cruising nonstop on this boat if I were the serious type? I'm so much more in a different place these days since I've been a widow, and I'm doing this to get away from real life." She placed her hand on my arm. "And trust me, my grown kids make life way too real for me. I feel sorry for my grandkids."

When we arrived at her cabin, she took me by the hand and pulled me inside. "Sit, Autumn. We need to figure out what's going on." So much for her not being serious.

"What did you hear?"

She pushed me into a chair and plopped down on the corner of her bed. "Aileen was getting a treatment, and she was telling someone else how she'd given a bad review."

"I didn't hear all of it, but I did hear the part about the bad review," I said. "I heard something about her and the other woman doing mystery shopping."

"That would be so much fun, don't you think?" Betty sighed. "I'll have to look into it after we finish this trip. If I can get even a week for free, I'm all for it. This traveling around the ocean so much is putting a serious dent in my bank account."

"But did you hear what they were saying? They think that's the reason they were poisoned."

"I don't think that's what they were saying at all."

"Don't you think it's too much of a coincidence that they're both mystery shoppers, and they both got sick?" I held out my hands. "What are the chances of that?"

Betty scrunched her face. "Yeah, maybe you're right, Autumn. We need to find out about those people who died. I wonder if they were mystery shoppers too."

"How can we find out?"

"I don't know. I was hoping you'd have some

ideas."

Maybe Summer would know. I didn't tell Betty about my cousin yet because I wasn't even sure if I wanted to call her again. First of all, it was getting really expensive, but secondly, I didn't want to bug her to death.

"I wonder if we should ask Aileen," Betty said. "The problem is she and I aren't exactly on the best of terms." She gave me a hopeful look. "Maybe you—" She stopped short and shook her head. "Never mind. I don't expect you to step out of your comfort zone and do anything like that. You're too ... well, you're just not the type to ask nosy questions."

"I can be as nosy as anyone," I argued. "But I'm not sure how wise that would be ... at least not now, considering the fact that Aileen and that other woman got poisoned. I'm afraid they'd think we did it."

"Why on earth would they think that?"

I shrugged. "They're probably suspicious of everyone."

"You're right." Betty's shoulders drooped. "I was just thinking how cool it would be if I was involved in helping to solve this mystery. You do realize that whoever figures it out will become a hero ... and maybe even have a movie made about them."

A light came on in my head. I already knew that Betty needed some attention, and now she saw a way to get it. If I could figure out what to do next, I'd hand her the baton and let her take credit.

I was about to tell her I'd try to come up with a plan when someone knocked on her cabin door. Betty gestured for me to keep quiet, but the person knocked again, only this time, harder.

"Betty, I know you're in there, and I know you're not alone. Let me in. I have to tell you something."

Chapter 15

Betty mouthed that it was Aileen, but I already knew that. I recognized her voice.

Aileen knocked again. "Please, Betty. Open up. This is a matter of life and death."

I nodded toward the door, so Betty walked over and opened it a few inches. Aileen didn't hesitate before pushing it all the way open and barging in.

"What are you doing here?" Betty asked. I heard her voice crack, so she wasn't nearly as tough as she was trying to sound.

"They're out to get us." Aileen's words gushed out on the edge of her breath.

I stood up. "Who's out to get you?"

Aileen shook her head, lifted her hands, and let them fall back to her sides, making a loud slapping sound. "How on earth would I know?"

"You're not making any sense, Aileen. Why don't you leave and come back when you have something to say?"

I lifted a finger to get their attention. "I have a better idea." I gestured toward the chair where I was sitting. "Why don't you have a seat, take a couple of deep breaths, and tell us what's going on and what's making you so scared?"

Betty frowned at me but didn't say anything as she resumed her position at the corner of her bed. After she realized I wasn't backing down about letting Aileen talk, she lowered her head to stare at something on the floor.

I turned back to Aileen. "Is someone chasing you?"

"Does it look like it?"

Betty's head shot up. "See? I don't know why you're being so nice to her, Autumn. All she's going to do is be a smart aleck."

"Look," Aileen said as she leaned forward and held out her hands. "I'm not trying to be a smart aleck or rude or whatever else it seems like I'm doing. You're right, Autumn. I'm ..." She let out a hiccup. "I'm scared."

Betty belted out a laugh. "You? Scared? Since when?"

Aileen pulled her lips between her teeth and shook her head. "I didn't want to tell anyone, but I've been ... well, I've been seeing a couple of the crew members."

"You've been seeing them?" Betty rolled her eyes. "What do you mean by that?"

"The captain and I started this thing last time I cruised."

Betty's eyes looked like they might pop right out

of her head. "You and the captain? Are you serious? I thought that was just a rumor." Betty gave me an incredulous look before glaring at Aileen. "You expect me to believe you and Thomas Myers are having a fling?"

"I didn't say we were having a fling. I just said we were seeing each other." She swallowed hard. "He makes me feel special."

"He does?" I wondered if Aileen realized that Betty already knew. I also wondered how what she was saying fit in with her mystery shopping.

Aileen nodded and then shrugged. "Well, he did. It's been a long time since I felt that way. We went out to dinner at a restaurant on the beach and danced to one of the local bands." She closed her eyes and swayed side to side, as though she was reliving her time with the captain. Then she opened her eyes as quickly as she'd fallen into her trance, and all the color drained from her face. "I think that time I spent with him has something to do with getting poisoned."

Betty gave me a smirk before focusing on Aileen. "You don't think it has anything to do with writing a bad report for your mystery shopping company?"

"What?" Aileen clearly appeared distraught. "What do you know about that?"

"I just happen to know that you and ... whatever that other woman's name is have been mystery shopping the cruise line." Betty gave her an evil grin. "Did you write about going off with Captain Myers and dancing the night away?"

"Never!" Aileen placed both of her hands over her

cheeks and squeezed her eyes shut. Then the tears started to fall.

"Oh no ya don't, Aileen. Don't start with the tears. I can't handle a wimpy, sobbing, pitiful woman."

"I can't help it. I'm just so …" Her face scrunched up like she was about to start into a full-blown sob, but she managed to stop. "I'm so upset and confused and distraught and—"

Betty held up her hands. "Okay, we get the picture. So you're afraid someone's after you. Do you have any idea who it might be?"

"There are several possibilities."

"I don't have all day," Betty said. "Just tell us."

"Well, first of all, I have to tell you about someone else."

"What are you talking about?" Betty looked at me as if expecting some support.

I blinked and focused on Aileen. "Someone else? Are you talking about someone who is out to get you or someone else you've been involved with?"

"I'm not involved with anyone, at least not now. I just happened to go out with a couple of the crew members—at different times, of course."

"Of course." Betty let out a little growl. "Just tell us who it is. I'm getting sick of this game you're playing."

"If you're going to act like that, I'm not telling."

Betty groaned and rolled her eyes. "Give me a break."

I decided to jump in with some of my own questions. "How serious were you and the captain?"

Aileen shook her head. "Not serious at all. Did you really think—?"

"Yes." The harsh sound of Betty's voice made me wince.

I realized I had to take over to keep Aileen talking. "So what about you and the captain?"

"As I already told you, he made me feel wonderful, but ever since Bertrand died, I haven't wanted to commit to anyone."

"Bertrand?" I tilted my head as I held her gaze. "Your husband?"

"No, my dog. My husband left me a long time ago, and I made the decision right after that to stay single and just get a dog."

"That's the most ridiculous thing I've ever heard." Betty turned to me. "Don't you agree, Autumn?"

I wasn't about to agree or disagree since I had no experience with long-term relationships ... or dogs. But I had to admit to myself that replacing a husband with a dog seemed a bit extreme.

Aileen held her arms out to her sides with her palms up. "So after Bertrand died ..." She squeezed her eyes shut and let another tear roll down her cheeks before looking back at me. "After my beloved Bertrand passed away, I've been going on cruises and train trips to keep my mind off of him and stay as busy as possible. It helps with the pain. When men ask me out, I go, but when things look like they might be getting serious, I cut things off. I don't want to put myself in such a vulnerable position, ever again."

Betty snorted. "So the death of your dog made

you turn to serial dating."

Looking at Aileen, it was difficult to wrap my mind around her dating the captain … or anyone else for that matter. She was an attractive but overly made up older woman, but she seemed more the grandmotherly type than a serial dater.

"Serial dating?" Aileen gave Betty a curious look. "What on earth do you mean by that?"

Betty bobbed her head. "Exactly what it sounds like. You don't want to commit, so you date one guy after another."

I held my breath, half expecting Aileen to explode, but she didn't. Instead, she laughed. "That's a new one on me. Like I said, I'm not exactly dating. I'm just stepping out with men for entertainment."

Betty held up her hands, palms facing Aileen. "I don't need to know the nitty gritty details." She paused. "So you're seeing these guys for …" She gave me a half smile before turning back to Aileen. "… for entertainment. And now you think someone wants to kill you for that?"

"I don't know for sure, but I wouldn't be surprised if that was somehow connected."

"Why would someone want to kill you, just because you're dating … er, stepping out with these guys?"

"The captain's wife—"

Now it was my turn to jump in. This was the first I'd heard about the captain being married, and that put a whole different light on things. "The captain's married, and you've been dating him?"

"I already told you, it's not dating. It's just *stepping out*. We went to dinner."

"And danced," Betty reminded her.

"But we never did anything else."

Now it was my turn to speak up. "Does the captain's wife ever come on these cruises?"

"She has in the past," Betty said. "She's actually quite a lovely woman."

"So you know her?" I asked.

She nodded. "I do. I'll tell you more about that later."

Aileen made a face as she pointed to our hands. "I see you ladies got your nails done. I hate those weird colors you girls chose. Why can't you just get them painted red like normal people?"

I was surprised when Betty didn't blow a gasket and laughed instead. "You sound just like Myrna."

Aileen and I both spoke in unison. "Who's Myrna?"

"Myrna Myers. We were just talking about her, remember?"

Aileen's eyebrows came together. "Tom's wife?"

Betty nodded. "I'd like to make a suggestion ... not that you'll take it or anything."

Aileen and I exchanged a glance and waited for Betty to continue. This conversation was slowly opening up some possibilities for suspects, and as interesting as it was, I was getting both excited and nervous about finding out who might want a bunch of people dead.

Betty leaned toward Aileen until she met her gaze.

"Stay. Away. From. The captain." She lifted her eyebrows. "Understand?"

"I don't see why you'd tell me to do that. I've already told you I'm not doing anything wrong."

The sound of more disorder in the hallway stopped our conversation. Betty hopped up, crossed the cabin, and opened the door. "Well, I'll be …"

Chapter 16

"Who is it?" Aileen stood and started to walk toward the door, but Betty waved her back. "What's going on, *Captain Myers*?" She emphasized his name, and I was pretty sure it was to give Aileen a reason to stand back. But it was too late.

"Oh, sorry. I didn't realize you had company. I can come back another time." The captain's voice sounded softer than I remembered—almost as though he were speaking to someone he personally cared about.

"My guests won't be here much longer. Can we talk up on the Lido Deck in an hour or so?"

The captain glanced at Aileen and me before turning back to Betty. "I thought we might need some privacy. Want me to come back here in an hour?"

"No." The clipped tone of Betty's voice alarmed me, and when I glanced at Aileen, I saw that she had the same reaction.

Aileen's eyes had narrowed to slits. She pursed her lips and shook her head after Betty closed the door and turned around to face us. Something about the look on Betty's face didn't seem right. She looked dazed ... and guilty.

"What's going on with you and Tom?" Aileen asked. "Are you seeing him and not telling us?"

"Why would you go and say something like that?" Betty's gaze darted around the room, as though she wasn't sure where to look.

"Well ..." Aileen took a couple of steps toward the door before turning around and addressing both of us. "Looks to me like a lot of fishy stuff is going on."

Betty contorted her mouth, but she didn't say anything. After Aileen left, Betty turned around to face me. "What do you think about all this?"

"It seems pretty complicated." I left out the fact that she appeared guilty of something.

She laughed. "That's what people say when they don't know what else to say."

"But it is, though, isn't it?"

Betty nodded. "I suppose so."

I didn't want to appear nosy, but my curiosity was getting the best of me, so I decided to just go for it. "Now that Aileen isn't here, do you want to tell me what's happening between you and the captain?"

She opened her mouth quickly but then clamped it shut just as fast as she sighed and sank back down on the corner of the bed. "Looks like you're smarter than I thought you were. And it looks like I can't pull anything over on you."

I probably shouldn't have taken credit for knowing something I didn't since it was just a wild guess based on her guilty expression, but I just sat there and waited for her to make a confession. Betty pursed her lips, swallowed a couple of times, and rubbed the back of her neck. She was clearly experiencing some intense discomfort.

"Okay, if you don't want to tell me, that's fine." I stood. "I understand."

"Wait. I'll tell you everything if you'll promise to keep it to yourself."

As tempting as it was to make that promise, I knew I couldn't withhold information that was illegal. "I'm sorry, Betty, but if someone is doing something that's against the law—"

"Oh, it's not against the law ... at least I don't think it is." She made another face as she squirmed. "Oh, all right, I'll tell you since you've probably already figured it out anyway."

I sat and waited as she summoned the courage. This was obviously more difficult for her than it was me, but I was still mighty uncomfortable.

"The reason I stay on this cruise is to keep an eye on my sister's husband."

"Your sister's husband?" I asked. "What does that have to do with—?"

She nodded. "Yeah, Tom Myers is married to my sister Myrna."

Betty couldn't have surprised me more if she'd jumped out of a cake wearing a bikini. "The captain is your brother-in-law?"

She smiled. "Yep. But there's a problem now."

I couldn't wait to hear about the next kink.

"What's the latest problem?"

"Well …" She pulled a tissue from her pocket and started fidgeting with it. "This is where it gets really messy. My sister and I have always been very close, but there have been times …" She grimaced.

"What kind of times?"

"She's a couple of years older than me, so she blazed the trails, and I followed. People saw her as the smart sister, the go-getter, someone with her head screwed on straight, while I was the baby and the one who needed to be taken care of. That bugged me to no end."

This was a side of Betty I'd never seen. "I can imagine. But you still haven't told me what the problem is."

"When Myrna met Tom, she came home and told me she'd met the man she was going to marry. I assumed she would get what she wanted because that's what always happened."

I lifted an eyebrow. "Okay, and the problem is?"

"She didn't tell me who he was, so I was in the dark for a couple of weeks until she brought him to meet me."

"You didn't like him?"

"Oh, quite the contrary. I liked him a lot." She gave me a sad smile. "In fact, I'd been dating him for several months."

I gasped. "Oh wow. You're full of surprises, Betty."

"That's because, unlike a lot of other people around here, I don't tell everything I know." She tipped her head forward. "And I'm not talking about you."

"So what exactly are you keeping an eye on the captain for?" I asked.

Betty waved her hand toward the door. "For what Aileen's doing. Myrna suspected there was some hanky panky, but she's not able to travel more than a couple times a year."

"Is she not well?"

"Oh, she's plenty well." Betty rolled her eyes. "It's just that she doesn't want to leave her precious little Poochie home alone too often."

"Poochie?"

"Her Peek-a-poo dog. She treats that animal like it's her child, and he's spoiled rotten. He even has his own bedroom with a canopy bed."

I've known people who pampered their pets, so I understood. "Do you report back on what you see?"

"To be honest, I don't really see all that much." She fidgeted some more. "Myrna pays half my fare, so I'm pretty much doing it for the money ... and as I mentioned, the opportunity to get away from my kids."

"Does she know that you used to date him?"

"Nope, and she's not gonna know either. I figure what she doesn't know won't hurt her."

"But a lot of time has passed, and you're sisters."

"I know. But don't forget she stole my man away and married him."

This was way more information than I ever needed or even wanted to know, but now I couldn't help myself. "So you're saying you never brought up the fact that you were dating him when she first introduced you?"

"That's exactly what I'm saying." Betty chuckled. "At first, he and I thought it would be fun to pretend we'd never met. And then things got serious between them when he found out she'd been married before and got a lot of money after her first husband died ... and at that point it didn't seem right." She glanced at the clock on her dresser. "You've been here a long time, Autumn."

"I know, and I was just thinking about going to my cabin. But I have one more question."

"Okay, I won't guarantee that I'll answer, but go ahead and ask."

"Do you have any thoughts about who might be poisoning people?"

Betty shook her head. "Nope." She stood up. "You need to leave now, Autumn. I need to get some rest."

I didn't need to be told twice. I had my hand on the doorknob when I heard Betty say my name, so I turned around to see what she wanted.

"You are not to tell a soul anything you heard in this room today." She narrowed her eyes and gave me a strong warning look that sent a creepy chill down my spine and up my arm. "Understand?"

"Yes, of course."

"Just making sure. Now you can go."

As I closed the door behind me, I spotted someone coming out of my cabin. "Hey, what are you doing in my room?"

I thought it was a man at first, but after the person turned around, I saw that his or her hair was tucked up in a hoodie. Instead of replying, the person took off running.

This was very unnerving, and I wasn't about to go in my cabin alone. I was afraid someone might still be in there. I didn't think Betty would want me to go back to hers, so I kept walking until I got to the elevator. I had to admit I was a little bit afraid to get on it alone, but I figured it was safer than going into a cabin that might still have an intruder.

I headed for the ship's office and saw someone I'd never noticed before sitting behind the desk. "Can I have someone from security check out my cabin?"

The woman tilted her head and frowned. "Why? Is something missing?" Before I replied, she pulled a clipboard out from beneath the desk and shoved it toward me. "Just fill out the top form, write down everything that's missing, sign it, and we'll take care of the rest."

"Nothing's missing ... or at least I don't know if anything's missing. All I know is someone was in my cabin."

She made a sour face. "If nothing's missing, how would you know someone was in there?"

"I saw him ... er, her coming out. I was down the hall."

"Which is it? A him or a her?" Now she had a mocking expression that got under my skin.

"I couldn't tell."

"If you can't see very well, how do you know it was your cabin?"

My frustration must have been evident because

she lifted her index finger to signal for me to wait, picked up the phone, and pressed some buttons. Less than a minute later, I heard someone behind me say my name.

Chapter 17

When I turned around, I saw the captain striding toward me. "What's this about someone being in your cabin?" The booming sound of his voice made my insides tighten.

I explained what I'd seen—and that I wasn't sure if it was a man or woman, and that I had no idea what the person looked like. He watched me with a look of apprehension.

"So do you want me to have someone go back with you?" His voice had softened quite a bit.

"Yes, I think so."

He turned to the woman behind the desk and told her to send someone to go back to my cabin with me. Then he faced me again with a troubled expression. "Someone will be here in just a few minutes. Were you planning to do anything else tonight?"

"No."

"Good. After your cabin is checked, lock the door and don't let anyone in."

"Okay."

He tilted his head forward with a look of concern. "And I mean it. Don't open your door for anyone, even if you think you know the person."

I held his gaze and slowly nodded. "I won't open it for a single person, regardless of who it is."

"You also need to stay mum about this. The fewer people who know what happened the better."

"I won't say a word to anyone."

"If you have any more trouble, call down here, and ask to be connected directly to me. I'll make sure you're okay."

"Thank you, Captain."

He started to walk away but stopped and turned back to face me. "Would you like to join me at the Captain's Table for dinner tomorrow night?"

"I'm not sure I'll be staying on the cruise." I gave him a contrite look. "I might be flying back home tomorrow."

A pained expression crossed his face. "I can certainly understand you wanting to do that, but it might not be easy to get a flight out on such short notice." He shifted his weight. "Tell you what. I'll leave the invitation open. If you're unable to get a flight, you're welcome to join me. I'd like to keep an eye on you since you've somehow gotten mixed up in this mess."

I'd always heard that it was an honor to be invited to the Captain's Table, and he was being awfully nice, but after what I'd recently learned about him, I wasn't so sure. I didn't want to offend the man in charge of the ship, so I swallowed hard and nodded.

He smiled. "You'll have to wear something nice. There'll be a big group at the table, and afterward, we'll have our pictures taken. And whoever would like can go on a private tour of some areas of the ship most passengers don't see." He paused. "And I'll make sure we have an extra crewmember with us."

I offered a weak smile and hoped that sometime between now and then I'd be well on my way home. But if that didn't happen, at least I'd be with a large group, which seemed somewhat safe.

Someone wearing a cruise ship officer's uniform arrived. Captain Myers explained what had happened and gave him instructions to check my room to make sure there was no one in there and nothing suspicious in my cabin. As soon as the captain left, the man gave me a long look.

"Thank you so much for coming down." I dug into my handbag, pulled out some cash, and handed it to him.

"No problem. You must have made quite an impression on the captain. He doesn't generally get involved with younger women."

"Oh, I'm sure he's just being a gentleman." I didn't want him to get the wrong idea and think there was anything between the captain and me.

"Captain Myers a gentleman?" He grinned and shook his head. "Now that's an interesting thought."

I took offense to this man talking about his boss in a disrespectful manner, so I decided not to continue to engage in conversation with him. He followed me to my cabin, looked under the bed, in the shower, and in the closet.

"Nothing looks out of line here," he said.

I glanced over at the desk and saw that there was a water pitcher beside my glass. "That wasn't there before."

"What wasn't?"

"That water pitcher."

He frowned. "Are you sure?"

"Positive."

"Don't touch it. I'll need to have someone investigate." He went into the bathroom, got some tissue, and used it to pick up the water pitcher. "I'll take this for fingerprints."

I walked him to the door and let him out since he had both hands on the water pitcher. "Thank you for checking things out."

"No problem." He walked out into the hallway and glanced over his shoulder. "Be careful, okay?"

"I will."

After I shut the door, I locked it and closed my eyes. I sure hoped I could get a flight out of St. Thomas tomorrow. This was wearing on me, and I was becoming more stressed out by the minute. In fact, I caught myself wishing I had school to go back to in order to get my mind off of this.

It took me a while, but I finally managed to go to sleep, and I had one dream after another. Not one of them made sense. When I finally awoke, I showered, dressed, and went out for breakfast. My nerves were on edge as I pondered what to eat at the buffet. I sure didn't want to take any chances.

So I decided on a cup of yogurt that was sealed and a banana. I brought it over to one of the chairs on the shady side of the Lido Deck. I'd just finished my yogurt when I sensed the presence of someone standing behind me.

I jerked around and let out a sigh of relief at the sight of Betty. She pointed to the chair beside me. "May I join you?"

"Sure."

"I heard about the excitement last night," she said.

Since I wasn't sure exactly what she was referring to, I didn't mention the person in my cabin. "Oh?"

She chuckled. "Don't pretend you don't know what I'm talking about. I know someone was in your cabin."

"How did you hear that?"

The smile never left Betty's face. "I'm friends with most of the crewmembers. The girl at the desk told me."

"Oh." I glanced down.

"Did they take anything?"

"I-I don't think so. At least I haven't noticed anything missing yet."

She pushed the top part of the lounge chair back and closed her eyes but kept talking. "I wonder what they wanted."

And I wondered if she knew and wasn't telling me. "I have no idea. I didn't bring any valuables on the cruise."

She opened her eyes, sat up, and turned to face

me. "You sure do have a lot to learn."

I gave her a curious look. "What do you mean?"

"What you don't consider valuable might be exactly what someone else wants." She paused. "Now do you get it, or do I have to spell it out for you?"

"I still don't think anything is missing."

"Just keep your eyes open and pay attention to everything." She leaned back, closed her eyes again, and kept talking. "We should be getting to St. Thomas soon. Are you still planning to fly out today?"

"I'm hoping to."

"You do realize it'll cost you an arm and a leg for airfare at this late time, right?"

Quite frankly, I didn't care if it cost my entire savings. I wanted to get away from the insanity on this ship and go home. "I figured it would be more expensive than it would have been if I planned it."

"Oh, honey, you just don't know." She opened one eye and offered a smile. "If you decide to stick around, you can hang out with me. I generally prefer to be alone, but you're actually kind of fun."

Betty's behavior puzzled me. First I annoyed her, and now I was fun? That didn't compute.

"I think I can teach you a few things," she continued.

"Teach me a few things?" I looked at her. "About what?"

"Different types of people, who to trust and who to be wary of ..." She shrugged. "And life in general."

"I know about life back in Nashville—" I stopped myself before adding that was the only life I wanted to know about, and I didn't ever want to leave the safe cocoon of my little world.

"There's a lot more to life than what you'll find in Nashville." She shifted her position on the chair. "I've been there a couple of times, and I have to admit, it's quite a nice place."

"It is," I agreed.

"My sister once told me that Nashville is as close to heaven as we'll ever get on this earth. I suppose it's all about what you consider heaven."

I started to talk about heaven and my faith, but she spotted something behind me that made her gasp. "I cannot believe who is coming this way."

Chapter 18

I started to look, but Betty grabbed my shoulder. "Don't turn around."

"Who is it?"

Her face had drained of all color, letting me know that she truly was surprised. "My sister. She never mentioned that she was coming on this cruise."

"Do you think she's been here the whole time?" I did my best to hide my shock, but I wasn't sure if I was successful.

"I have no idea." Betty's chest rose and fell as she took a deep breath and blew it out. "But I'll know soon. That girl has some explaining to do."

"Well, hello there, Betty. Mind if I join you and your little friend?"

Now I figured it was safe to look up. She smiled down at me with a vacant expression. I could tell she'd had some work done because nothing on her face moved but her lips.

"Have a seat." Betty glanced at me and then at her

sister.

"And what's your name, dear?"

"That's rude, Myrna." Betty scowled at her sister. "Autumn, this is my sister Myrna."

"Nice to meet you, Autumn." She chuckled without smiling past her lips that were a tad too plumped up. "What kind of name is that? Are your parents hippies?"

I didn't have a chance to respond before Betty spoke up again, this time looking at me. "I'm so sorry for my sister's rudeness. She got like this later in life. We certainly weren't raised that way."

"That's okay." I turned toward Myrna. "No, my parents aren't hippies. After my mother's sister named her daughter Summer, my parents thought it would be fun to have another season in the family ... you know, for balance."

"That sounds awfully silly to me, but I'll take your word for it." Myrna turned her attention back to her sister. "So how's your cruise going, sis?"

"Tom never told me you were on the boat," Betty said.

A strange look flashed through Myrna's eyes, but it was difficult to read since her facial muscles appeared frozen. "That's because he doesn't know."

"How did you—?"

"I have my ways." Myrna shifted in the chair. "But he'll know soon enough. I plan to show up at the Captain's Dinner tonight to surprise him." Her lips smiled again. "It should be interesting to see his reaction."

"Oh, it'll be interesting, all right." Betty flashed a glance in my direction.

I looked back and forth between the sisters. While there was a slight resemblance in skin tone and mannerisms, I wouldn't have guessed that they were sisters if I didn't know.

Myrna narrowed her gaze as she looked at me, clearly trying hard to ignore Betty. "So how do you like cruising, Autumn?"

I wasn't sure how much she knew about what was going on with the poisonings, and I didn't want to be the one to tell her, so I decided to take a noncommittal approach. "It's fine."

"Oh, come on, Autumn," Betty said. "This girl is ready to jump ship. In fact, she's planning to get the next flight out of St. Thomas."

"That might be difficult." Myrna shook her head. "For one thing, this is tourist season, and I've heard others have tried but to no avail."

A sinking sensation washed over me. "Maybe I can get on standby."

"You might be able to, but it's a huge risk. You don't want to get off the ship, have it leave, and wind up stranded in St. Thomas for who knows how long. Even if you can find a room, which I doubt that you'll be able to, they're very pricy right now."

Betty grimaced. "Yeah, I wondered about that."

"Why are you so bent on leaving? Is the service terrible? Are you seasick?"

Once again, Betty spoke for me. "She's worried about all the craziness that's been happening lately.

Did you know that Aileen was just about poisoned to death?"

"Aileen Graves?" Myrna feigned shock. I could tell she wasn't surprised, which raised a red flag.

Betty snorted. "Who else would I be talking about?"

"Where is she ... I mean, did the coroner come and take her away?"

Betty and I exchanged a glance. I could see that she was trying to give me a message in her expression, but since I couldn't tell what it was, I decided to remain silent until I figured it out.

"I'm not sure where Aileen is." Betty didn't look directly at me as she spoke. "Now tell me, sis. How on earth did you get onboard this ship without Tom knowing?"

Myrna bobbed her head. "I have my ways."

"Yes, you certainly do," Betty mumbled as she turned to me. "Autumn, you'd better watch out for this one. She's sneaky."

"I beg your pardon. You've always been the sneaky one."

"Nope. You are much sneakier than I ever have been."

"Not in this lifetime." Myrna looked at me. "She's the sneaky sister." She glanced at Betty. "Remember when I had a bunch of friends over, and you hid in my closet the whole time?"

Betty closed her eyes and shuddered. "Yeah, the things I saw and heard—"

"We had no idea you were in there until you told

Mom what we were doing. And we got in so much trouble."

"If you didn't want to get in trouble, you shouldn't have done that."

Now my curiosity had gotten the best of me. "What were y'all doing?"

Betty opened her mouth but quickly closed it. Myrna spoke up instead.

"Just normal stuff teenage girls do. The only reason we got in trouble was Mom wanted to set an example for my baby sister to make sure she didn't do the same thing."

Since it was obvious that they weren't going to tell me what they were talking about, all I could do was use my imagination. I didn't do anything terribly bad as a kid, but I'd heard plenty from my students.

Betty stood up and stretched. "Why don't we take this conversation back to my cabin? You're likely to be discovered out here on deck."

Myrna nodded as she lifted her scarf and draped it over her head and around her shoulders. "Let's go."

"Autumn, you stay here," Betty said. "I have to discuss a few things with my sister, and I'd hate for you to be put in the middle of it. There's a lot of dirt we have to talk about."

I nodded. Even though I was still curious, I was relieved that she cared enough to keep me out of whatever *dirt* they needed to discuss.

"And don't you dare tell a soul I'm here," Myrna added.

I gulped hard. "Okay, I promise I won't say a word

to anyone about you."

A smile replaced her steely gaze. "Good girl."

~

An hour later, we arrived at St. Thomas. My heart pounded with anxiety about finding a way to get off this crazy ship and go back home. As I wheeled my suitcase off the ship, people stared at me.

Unfortunately, when I got to the airport, I discovered it was just as bad as Myrna had said. Not only did they not have any openings on flights, they were overbooked for the next several days and not likely to be able to seat those who'd already gotten reservations.

I walked around in a daze for another couple of hours, dragging my suitcase behind me, before returning to the ship. There were some tours that I could have joined, but at this point, I wasn't in the mood.

As I boarded, I saw the captain talking to some of the passengers, so I darted by as quickly as possible, hoping I wouldn't be noticed. I thought I made it, but the sound of someone calling my name brought a feeling of dread.

I turned around and spotted Andrea walking toward me, smiling. "I heard you were planning to leave the cruise." She glanced down at my suitcase.

"All the flights are booked, so it looks like I'll be staying."

"If there's anything I can do to make your cruise more enjoyable, let me know. It bothers all of us when a passenger isn't happy." She narrowed her gaze, gave me a look I couldn't read, and then widened her eyes. It seemed as though she was trying to tell me something without saying whatever it was.

"It's not you. It's just that ..." I wasn't sure what to say since the poisoning was supposed to be a secret, and I didn't know if the cruise director was privy to everything that was going on. I suspected she knew, but I wasn't taking any chances on being the one to spill the beans.

"Why don't you join some of the crew at the party tonight after dinner? We have a few extra spots at our table."

"What kind of party?"

"It's a celebration of everything—birthdays, anniversaries, retirement, vacation, whatever. Everyone here has a reason to celebrate something."

"Maybe." I didn't feel like celebrating, but the only other option I saw was to go to my room after dinner.

"C'mon, it's fun."

"I don't know ..."

"Think about it." She lowered her voice. "I'd love for someone closer to my age to join us. Since I've been on this ship, I've felt like the odd woman out."

That touched me. "Okay, maybe I will join you."

She flashed a genuine smile. "I can't even begin to tell you how happy I am about that. I have a feeling you and I could be good friends in any other situation."

My heart went out to her. She was one of the few female crewmembers on the boat, and the others were at least as old as my mother.

She jotted down all the information and handed it

to me so I'd know where to go. "Try to get there early if you can. I want to make sure we're able to sit next to each other."

I walked away feeling a little bit better. At least I had something to look forward to now.

The hallways were mostly empty as I made my way to my cabin. I'd heard other passengers and some of the crewmembers call them corridors, but to me they were narrow hallways.

As soon as I unlocked my cabin door, a chill ran down my spine. Standing right in front of me, a few feet away from my closet was Aileen. She spun around and gave me a horrified look, and I could tell she was as surprised as I was.

Chapter 19

"What are you doing here?" she asked. "I thought you were flying out when we got to St. Thomas."

"Who told you that?" I glanced around my cabin to see if she'd moved anything. "But more important, what are *you* doing here?"

Her shoulders sagged as she sank down on the edge of the bed. "I was hoping to find someplace to hide."

"Why here?"

She shrugged. "I figured no one would think to look for me here, and I thought you weren't coming back."

"Were you planning to stay here for the remainder of the cruise?" I asked.

She nodded. "That was the plan."

"How did you get in?"

"I have my ways." She propped her elbows on her knees and lowered her face into her hands.

"Just tell me how you got in here." I glared at her.

"If you don't, I'll have to report you."

"Okay, okay. I came in when housekeeping was here."

"Did they let you in?"

She shook her head. "No, I waited until they were almost finished, and then when they weren't looking, I ran inside and hid in the closet until they left."

I wasn't sure if I believed her, but her word was all I had at the moment. And now I had to figure out what to do.

Her chin quivered, and a tear trickled down her cheek. "I guess you want me to leave."

Her expression tugged at my heart, but I couldn't let her get to me. I nodded. "That would be nice."

"Can I stay here just a little while longer? I'm afraid to go to my cabin."

"Why are you afraid?"

"I'm pretty sure I saw Myrna, the captain's wife, and she doesn't like me at all. I'm worried she might be after me." She paused. "But it might not have been her. I'm not sure."

I didn't want to tell her that Myrna definitely was onboard or anything else I knew. "Why don't you just stay in your own cabin and not go anywhere?"

"Because they know where to find me. No one would think to look for me here."

I tilted my head. "Is there anyone else you're worried about finding you?"

She lowered her gaze. "Just Myrna."

"But you weren't sure it was her."

"If it was, I can't let her see me."

"Okay, so what if she does find you? What do you think she'll do?"

"I don't know. That woman's crazy."

"How do you know that?" I asked.

"Tom told me so. He's been trying to divorce her for years, but she won't give him up."

"Are you sure about that?"

She jutted her chin and nodded. "He told me, and I believe him."

"Why would he tell you he wanted to divorce his wife?" I thought about Betty's comment regarding the money Myrna had, and I suspected that might be the glue holding the marriage together.

Aileen looked at me like I'd lost my mind. "Seriously? You have to ask?"

She was in my room, which made me feel like I had the upper hand for a change. "Yes, and I want you to tell me, or I'll have to let someone know you broke into my cabin." I picked up the phone to drive my point home.

A scowl came over her face. "I can't believe I'm having to explain the obvious. Tom and I have been in love for a long time."

"But you said—"

"Never mind what I said. This is the truth."

That sort of explained a few things, but I still had some questions. "Do you think that was why you were poisoned?"

"Of course. Why else would someone try to kill me?"

"I suppose you think that person is Myrna."

She nodded again. "That goes without saying."

I pondered that for a moment. "Are you sure she knows about you?"

She lifted her chin and leveled me with a look of defiance. "He told me she does."

"And you believe everything he tells you?"

"Of course. Why would he lie to me?"

"I don't know." He obviously didn't mind being unfaithful if what Aileen said was true, so I doubted a lie here and there would bother his conscience. "Something doesn't seem right here."

Aileen had put me in a very awkward position. If she was right and Myrna wanted to murder her, I'd be smack dab in the middle of it if I couldn't get rid of Aileen. She absolutely couldn't stay in my cabin, or I feared that I might get caught in the crossfire if something went down.

"What am I supposed to do?"

I sighed and shook my head. "I don't know what you should do, but I do know you can't stay here."

"Okay, I'll leave your cabin." Aileen walked over to the door and placed her hand on the knob. Before opening it, she turned to face me. "If something happens to me, it'll be on your conscience."

"Stay out of trouble," I said. "Don't go near the captain, and for heaven's sake, stay away from anyone who resembles his wife, if you think she wants to get rid of you."

Aileen made a clicking sound with her tongue. "You sure do have a lot to learn, Autumn." She hesitated only for a couple of seconds before leaving me alone in my cabin.

As soon as she was gone, I turned the lock and wedged a chair beneath the doorknob. Then I sat down in the nearest chair and pondered what to do next.

I wished I hadn't already spent so much time talking to Summer, but she helped me sort through everything. I still needed to chat with her again, now that more had transpired since our last phone call. Without hesitation, I pulled out my phone and called her.

She answered on the first ring. "I was hoping you'd call again. What's going on now?" The eagerness in her voice was obvious, and that made me smile.

I told her as quickly as I could, and somehow she managed to follow along. "This is one of those times I feel completely helpless … even more than when an entire class of seventh graders decides to plan a mutiny."

Summer laughed. "You'll be fine." Her voice grew more somber. "But from the sound of things you do need to be extra cautious, now that you're getting close. Strange stuff happens when the killer gets scared. Do you have any idea … any feeling about who might be doing this?"

"Feeling?"

"Yeah, like those goose-bump-up-the-arm moments when you're around certain people?"

"I've had several of those." I reflected back on a few times when I knew something wasn't right before I actually saw it. "And it's not just around one person. There are several."

"You have to trust that feeling," Summer said. "One of the biggest problems with people is that they try to ignore the instincts God gave them."

"But what if I'm wrong? I'd feel really silly for overreacting."

"It's better to be wrong and feel silly than to ignore what could be the biggest hint and get yourself into trouble … or worse, get hurt or killed. Do you think Myrna might be the person trying to murder people? She's the one with the most obvious motive."

"I thought about that as soon as I saw her."

"And you couldn't tell who that person was in your cabin … the one who ran away?" She paused. "Do you know the person's height?"

"I still have no idea who it was, but the person seemed a tad on the short side. It's so strange, though. I wonder why someone would break into my room, just to put a pitcher of water on the desk. I suppose I'll find out more when they check for fingerprints."

Summer sighed. "Don't count on it. From the sound of things, they're not likely to find definitive fingerprints, and if they do, they probably won't tell you much of anything."

"I thought fingerprints would be a good clue."

"A lot of people think that. Unfortunately, all kinds of things can muddle the results—from more than one person handling the pitcher to smudges." She paused. "And then there's always the chance that the person was wearing gloves to prevent detection. Most people have watched enough mysteries on TV to know how that works."

"You used to say that most of what detectives do on TV isn't accurate."

She laughed. "The key word being *most*. They normally get the fingerprints right, but not always."

"There has to be a clue."

"There always is. Are you sure it's cyanide?"

"That's what I keep hearing people talking about."

"Cyanide is rather old fashioned, and it doesn't always kill people who ingest it. In fact, a lot of fruits have cyanide in their seeds"

I shuddered. "Now I don't want to eat fruit anymore."

Summer laughed. "Don't get all paranoid. You've probably ingested some cyanide and didn't even realize it."

"That's horrible. Okay, now I feel worse."

"Seriously, Autumn, you need to just pay attention to everything. Be careful what you say and don't take any chances when you go back to your cabin. It's important to know if someone is in your room before you go inside. You know about the paper-in-the-door trick, right?"

"What are you talking about?"

"It doesn't prevent an intruder, but it'll let you know if someone has been in your cabin."

"How does that work?" I asked.

Chapter 20

"What you do is get a very small piece of paper and stick it in the door. When it opens, it'll fall to the floor. So before you open the door, check to see if the paper is still there. You'll have to make sure that you can see it from outside your cabin without making it too obvious."

"Won't an intruder see it?"

"Maybe, but if it's small enough, they'll have to consciously look for it. Don't have it sticking out where someone who doesn't know to look for it will see it."

"That sounds too easy."

Summer laughed. "I know, right? There are other things you can do to know if someone has entered the room, but none of them will stop anyone who really wants to get inside."

"What's another way to know?"

"If you have baby powder, you can put a little bit on the inside and outside knob. Anyone who touches it will leave a smudge."

"Thanks, Summer. I wish you were here with me."

"So do I. This is the kind of thing that excites me, which is why I'm still thinking about going back into law enforcement."

"I bet your mom will have the big one."

"Actually she's fine with it. At first, they didn't want me to, but now they're thinking I was better off doing that for a living since I still keep finding dead bodies. Dad said he likes the idea of my having a partner and constant backup—something I don't get as a civilian. They worry about me more now than they did when I was an active officer of the law."

"So that's not just talk … you're really thinking about going back, huh?"

"Yeah. Everything else bores me to tears. I've tried everything from office work to being a day care worker. That actually wouldn't have been too bad if I didn't get so mad at the parents. The kids were great."

"Maybe you and I can take a trip somewhere before you go back," I said.

She laughed. "If you're having trouble with what you're dealing with now, you definitely don't want to take a vacation with me. You're guaranteed to find a dead body, and of course, that means I won't be able to go home until I find the killer."

"In that case, you're right. We can take separate vacations and get together later for dinner and talk about it."

After we got off the phone, I settled down to ponder what to do next. Summer has always had a way of making me feel like everything will turn out fine while I'm talking to her, but later, I remember that I don't have her skills, and the small amount I know can get me into trouble and worry me to pieces.

I stayed in my cabin until my stomach started rumbling, letting me know it was time to eat. How people could fast for days and days I'd never know.

After experiencing a couple of intruders on this trip already, I decided to try Summer's paper-in-the-door method of security. I tore a small strip of paper from the scratch pad on the dresser and stuck it in the door as I left, making sure it didn't show too much from the outside but I could see it when I stood right in front of it and squinted my eyes. Then I made my way to one of the buffets. I would have gone to the dining room, but I wasn't in the mood to make conversation with a bunch of people at my assigned table.

There was hardly anyone out and about. Even during the dinner hour, there were typically a few people strolling around on the Lido Deck. However, tonight, I was one of only a couple of people, which concerned me because I wondered if they'd even bother with the buffet.

When I rounded the corner, I let out a sigh of relief. The buffet table was filled to overflowing with fresh fruit, shrimp on ice, and a colorful array of veggies. I made a beeline to it but stopped when I heard my name.

I spun around and saw Betty watching me, so I smiled. "Hey, Betty. I thought you'd be in the dining room. Did you get switched to a different seating?"

She didn't even try to smile back. Instead, she

nodded toward the buffet table. "I'd be careful eating any of that if I were you. You never know what might be in it."

Those goose bumps Summer and I talked about started crawling up my arm. I tried hard to ignore them since I doubted Betty had it in her to kill anyone. She might have been annoying, but I didn't think she was a murderer. "You think there might be something with poison on it, huh?"

She shrugged. "Maybe. Whoever's doing this is starting to get desperate."

My stomach hissed at me, reminding me it was time to eat, but my sense of wanting to stay alive took over. I backed away from the buffet table.

"Or it could be perfectly fine." She looked at it and then at me. "Tell you what. We'll both have the buffet. That way, we won't have to die alone." She let out a cackle before nudging me in the side. "Lighten up, Autumn. Where's your sense of humor?"

My sense of humor didn't find this conversation the least bit funny. I decided to change the subject.

"So why aren't you having dinner in the dining room?"

Betty rolled her eyes. "I'm tired of looking at the same old faces. Sometimes I think I've been on this boat way too long." She paused. "Know what I mean?"

I nodded. I'd only been on the boat a few days, and I felt I'd been there too long. I couldn't imagine staying on it for two years.

"I heard the pineapple is really good." Betty stabbed a couple of spears before moving on to the shrimp. "And I can't resist boiled shrimp." She piled a bunch of shrimp on her plate. "Did you know this is an all-you-can eat buffet?"

"Yes." I looked everything over and decided to get what Betty got. My reasoning was that if someone wanted to poison the food they'd choose something that didn't have a shell on it. And if Betty was the person poisoning people, she wouldn't pick anything that was tainted.

After we filled our plates, I picked up some bottled water and walked over to one of the tables with a striped umbrella. Betty was right behind me.

"You know they don't normally have this much stuff on the buffet at this time, right?" Betty picked up a piece of pineapple, studied it for a few seconds, and stuck it in her mouth.

"No, I didn't know that. I wonder why they do now."

"I'm sure they had an abundance of extra food since so many people canceled their reservations." Betty peeled a shrimp, dipped it in cocktail sauce, and popped it into her mouth. Her eyes rolled back as she chewed. "Mmm. That is so good. Beats prime rib any day."

"Is that what they're serving?"

Betty nodded. "That's one of several things on the menu. It's getting boring to keep having the same menu over and over. I tried to talk them into changing things up, but they told me they have their menu down to a science, and they're not about to change things up for just one passenger who doesn't want to leave the ship."

"Who told you that?" I couldn't imagine anyone with this cruise line being so blunt.

"Tom." She laughed. "He can get away with saying stuff like that to me." She lifted her fork but paused it a couple of inches from her lips. "Wait a minute. I thought you were supposed to have dinner at the Captain's Table tonight."

"I changed my mind."

"Tom won't like that one single bit." She tipped her head forward and gave me a look my mother used to give me. "Did you tell him you wouldn't be there?"

"I sent him a message through the front desk."

"He'll probably never get it." She snorted. "This cruise line has gone downhill since my first cruise. Take the cruise director, for instance."

"Are you talking about Andrea?"

Betty nodded. "That girl is such a flake."

"Since she's new, maybe he won't—"

Betty interrupted me. "Being new is no excuse. She should be able to step into the job knowing what to do." She shook her head and clicked her tongue. "I don't know why they hire such ditzy people."

"She seems nice to me." I thought back to the times I'd spoken with her, and I couldn't remember a single incident of flakiness.

"Oh, she might seem nice, but there's a side to her you'll probably never see." She leaned forward and whispered, "There's some speculation she and the Doc Healey are involved."

"Involved?" I put down my fork. "As in a

relationship?"

"Yep. And that's not all. She's been known to sabotage people when she doesn't get her way."

"She has?" I tilted my head. "I thought she was new."

"This started on her first day on the job. There's something odd about that girl, and I haven't figured it out yet." She lifted her index finger as if to make a point. "But mark my word, I will someday."

"Maybe there's nothing to figure out."

"Oh, trust me there is." Betty leaned toward me, cupped her hand, and whispered, "She might even have something to do with what's been happening." She bobbed her head. "Just sayin' ..."

I couldn't see that at all. "Maybe it just seems that way."

"Goodness, Autumn, you are even more naïve than I thought. Have you always been that way?"

"I like to look for the good in people."

"But some people haven't got an ounce of good in them—even some folks who pretend. You need to stop looking at the world through rose colored glasses."

The mother of one of my students told me that during my first year of teaching. It wasn't long after that when I became more realistic about the fact that most of the seventh graders in my classes weren't eager little sponges, hoping to soak up knowledge.

Betty tipped her head to the side and squinted her eyes as she stared at me. "What are you thinking about that's making you look so goofy?"

I chuckled. "My students."

"Stop thinking about those brats. You're supposed to be on vacation, remember?"

"They're not all brats." I might have had a rough year, but I hated when someone said something not so nice about my students.

"Oh yeah? I've never met a kid yet who wasn't."

I thought about some of the sweeter kids, like Danielle who turned all of her homework in on time and never once gave me a lick of trouble … and Anna who liked telling me funny jokes when she saw that I was having a rough day.

After I remained silent for a while, Betty spoke up again. "I reckon there might be some nice kids, but like I said, I haven't seen them. Maybe it's just all the ones who come cruising are a bunch of spoiled brats. Their parents should leave them at home with sitters."

"Is that what you did?" I asked.

"Yeah, pretty much. By the time school was out every year, I was ready for the loony farm. My late husband and I took them to their grandmother's house, and that was when we really lived it up."

"Did y'all go on cruises?"

Betty shook her head. "He didn't like anything to do with the water. He was more of a mountain man." She looked off in the distance with a dreamy expression. "A couple of years we went abroad—once to Japan and then another time to Europe." She shrugged. "Other times we just rented a place in the mountains. He fished all day, and I read."

It bothered me that she couldn't wait to get away from her children, but there was nothing I could do about it now. "Which did you like better, Japan or Europe?"

"I preferred Japan, but my husband liked Europe." She snorted. "His favorite tourist place was the Nestle factory in Switzerland. Of course, it was in the mountains, and he was a chocoholic."

"It makes sense that he would like it." I agreed.

Our conversation went on like that until her eyes widened, and she dropped her fork. There was clearly something behind me, and I wasn't sure whether or not I should turn around.

Chapter 21

"Betty, we'd like to have a chat with you."

I recognized Aileen's voice, so I looked over my shoulder, and I almost dropped my fork too. Now I knew why Betty was so shocked. Not only was Aileen standing there, Myrna was right beside her. Neither of them wore even a hint of a smile.

"Okay, so chat." Betty's voice cracked, so she cleared her throat.

Myrna looked down at me. "We'd like some privacy, please."

"Sure." I started to stand, but Betty yanked me by the arm, throwing me off balance. Fortunately the chair was right behind me, so I didn't have far to fall.

"Anything you have to say to me, say it in front of my friend." Betty gave me a quick glance.

"This is something I don't think you want her to hear." Myrna's jaw tightened as she glared at her sister. "It's serious stuff, Betty." She spoke with a low growl that made my skin crawl.

Betty's eyes narrowed, and her mouth formed a straight line as she looked at Myrna and then Aileen before dropping her gaze to mine. Finally, she nodded. "Why don't you go somewhere, Autumn? My sister and this other woman won't leave us alone if you don't."

"Or you can come with us, Betty," Aileen said. "Don't punish Autumn for being in the wrong place at the wrong time. She has every right to relax on deck."

"That's okay." I got up again, only this time no one tried to stop me. "I have stuff to do anyway."

Before anyone could say another word, I hightailed it back toward my cabin. I'd barely rounded the last turn when I ran into Andrea.

Her face lit up in a smile. "I was just looking for you. I didn't see you at dinner, and the captain said you were supposed to be at his table if you weren't able to get a flight out." She paused. "Then someone said they saw you come back on the ship, so I got worried."

I explained what I did. "I'm not really up to any kind of celebration right now."

"I understand, but maybe you can at least come for a little while." She shrugged as she continued smiling. "And who knows. Maybe it'll cheer you up. This is my favorite event on all the cruises."

I wasn't in the mood to be cheered up, but I also knew I'd sound like a curmudgeon for saying that. "I don't know."

"Please?" Her forehead scrunched as she begged. "Just for half an hour? If you hate it, you can come back to your cabin. It'll make the whole crew feel better if you do."

Half an hour wouldn't be too bad, I figured. I could endure almost anything for that long.

"Okay, I'll go for a little while, but I really don't want to stay long."

She gave me a clipped nod and a satisfied expression. "Understood."

"I need to change first."

She looked me up and down. "You don't really *have* to change."

I laughed. "Well, since you put it that way, I really want to. It's the least I can do since I didn't show up at the Captain's Table."

Andrea tilted her head and looked at me from beneath her perfectly manicured eyebrows. "Would you like for me to wait for you?"

"I don't want to keep you from your work."

"That's okay. I don't have to account for my time right now." She let out a giggle. "Contrary to what some people think, we do have a little bit of free time during cruises."

"Okay, if you want to hang out, that's fine with me."

We went into my cabin, and she plopped down on the chair and took off her shoes. "My feet are killing me."

I glanced at the stilettos she'd kicked off. "Why do you wear such high heels?"

"Because I'm five-foot-two, and I hate being patted on the head."

"Tell you what." I pulled out a long black skirt and loose-fitting top. "I'll wear flats, so if you want to change shoes, you won't be the only short person at the party."

"You're such a sweet person," she said. "I bet you have a bunch of friends back home."

"I have a few." I thought about the people I called friends and realized most of them were acquaintances. "But just a couple of really close pals."

"Same here. After I got out of high school, everyone scattered to different colleges and jobs. Then after college, I lost track of so many people."

"Do you have a Facebook page? That's how I keep track of all the people who moved away from Nashville."

She nodded. "I do, but in case you haven't noticed, Internet onboard the ship can be quite sketchy, and cell phone service isn't much better."

I finished getting everything I needed. "I'll get ready in the bathroom. It'll only take a couple of minutes."

"Take your time." She leaned back, propped her feet on the ottoman, and folded her hands in her lap. "I'll just enjoy a few minutes of quiet."

I smiled at her as I closed the bathroom door. After hanging my skirt and top on the door hook, I thought of something I forgot to ask. So I opened the door, and to my dismay, she had her back to me as she was standing in front of my open suitcase and rummaging around. I quickly closed the door, carefully turning the knob so she wouldn't be able to hear the click.

What on earth could she possibly hope to find in my things? I didn't have anything worth worrying about, but the very thought of someone digging through my stuff bugged me.

I slowly changed into my skirt and top. And right before I opened the door, I coughed to make sure I didn't catch her doing anything she didn't want me to see. When I walked out of the bathroom, she was back in the chair, looking relaxed. I glanced over at my suitcase and saw that she'd closed it. I'd left it open.

When I turned back to her, I saw a look of shock on her face. She probably figured out what I'd noticed, so I started talking about something to get her mind off of it. Fortunately, she took the bait.

I managed to keep the conversation light as we made our way to the elevator. I offered to go along with her to her cabin to get some comfy shoes, but she said she had some in her office. After stopping off so she could pick up her flats, we went to the party that was in full swing.

The first thing I did was to find the captain so I could apologize for not making it to his table. He gave me a cursory nod and half smile, said it was okay, and walked away. Okay, so he was annoyed, but at least I tried to make things right.

For the next half hour, regardless of who I talked to, all I could think about was Andrea going through my suitcase. When I saw her talking to Aileen, I noticed a different expression on her face. In fact, they seemed awfully close and in tune with each other—almost as though they had some special connection.

Someone had started handing out party noisemakers. I accepted one, but I stuck it in my pocket since I had no intention of using it. The party was raucous enough as it was.

I finally decided I'd had enough, and it was time to leave. I approached Andrea. "I'm really tired. I think I'll go back to my—"

"No." Her loud abruptness startled me, but she dropped her voice down a notch. "I mean you can't go yet. The party hasn't gotten started."

"I'm really not much of a party girl, and the noise—"

Before I had a chance to finish my sentence, she grabbed me by the arm and led me to a quieter area. "How's this?"

"Better." I glanced around. "But I still want to go to my cabin."

"Please stay." She tilted her head and gave me a puppy dog look. "I really don't like being the only person our age here."

"There are some younger people over there." I pointed to a couple standing over by the captain. "Why don't you talk to them?"

"Because they're a couple, and I'm ... well, you know ..." She tilted her head and gave me another one of her pleading expressions.

If I hadn't caught her rifling through my things, I might have taken pity on her, but something didn't seem right about this whole situation. And of course, I totally didn't trust her or anything she said.

"Andrea!" The sound of a masculine voice caught both of our attention, and we turned around to see Doc Healey coming toward us, appearing as though he was on a mission. "I've been looking all over for you."

Chapter 22

She took a step toward the doctor, but when I tried to follow, she lifted a hand. "You stay right here. I'll be back."

I did as she requested, but I was annoyed about it. The two of them had serious looks on their faces as they stood very close to each other and spoke. I wondered if something had happened to another passenger.

As I waited, I watched the partiers, as they seemed to be having a great time. I wished there was some sort of magic volume button so I could turn down the noise. My head felt as though it might explode with the next drumbeat.

Finally, after what seemed like forever but was probably only five minutes, Andrea came back toward me, a plastic smile on her face. "The doctor said he'd like to chat with you." She leaned closer. "He thinks you're very attractive."

"Thank you, but I really need to head back to my

cabin." Instead of waiting for her to argue, I turned around and started for the door.

Somehow the doctor made it to the door before me, and he stood there, grinning, arms folded, and his feet shoulder width apart. "Don't tell me you're leaving so soon." He winked. "It's still early … the night is young."

"I'm sorry, but I'm not much of a night person." I tried to sidestep him, but he was faster than me. I forced a smile. "Please. I'm really tired."

He glanced at something behind me before finally letting out a deep sigh. "Okay, if you must go. I'm just disappointed that we haven't had a chance to get to know each other."

"Maybe some other time."

He offered a tender smile, belying his demeanor from a few minutes ago. "Yes, some other time when you're more rested."

As I exited, I managed to glance over my shoulder to see what or who he'd been looking at, and I saw that he was already deep in conversation with Andrea again. Before I had a chance to duck out of sight, the doctor made eye contact with me and nodded. Andrea glanced up so quickly I felt like a deer in headlights.

I started to my cabin, but before I got to the elevator, I heard Andrea calling my name. "Wait up."

My heart sank as I kept going, pretending not to hear her. All I wanted to do was be alone in my cabin, away from the insanity on this ship.

Once I got to my cabin, I let out a sigh of relief. I went over to my suitcase and hesitated for a few seconds as I thought about how I'd seen Andrea looking through my things. When I lifted the top, I was surprised by how organized everything still seemed— just as I'd left it.

That fact made me take a step back and wonder about Andrea. Betty was right. There was definitely something different about her, but I couldn't put my finger on what it was. When she and Doc Healey had their heads together, talking a few minutes ago, I'd noticed a familiarity that went beyond the coworker relationship. I wondered what was going on between them and if they had a romantic relationship. But then if that were the case, why wouldn't it bother Andrea to know that he'd asked me out to dinner, and why would she tell me he thought I was attractive. There was obviously a clue here that I couldn't wrap my mind around.

My first thought was to call Summer and tell her the latest, but I thought about how my charges kept mounting up. Then I considered the fact that there was no amount of money I could put on safety, and this whole situation felt about as unsafe as it could get.

She didn't even let the phone finish the first ring this time before answering. And she started talking without even saying *hello*. "I've been doing some checking around, and I found out some stuff that might interest you."

I cleared my throat. "Like what?"

"Like the fact that the cyanide tests came back on those people who died, and they found other elements that they're investigating. Did you know that a lot of foods naturally have cyanide?"

"You already told me a lot of fruit seeds have it." I thought for a moment. "And I sort of remember one of my students saying not to chew apple seeds because they have cyanide."

"But you'd have to eat an awful lot of apple seeds to get enough cyanide to kill you."

"What other foods have it?" I asked.

"Well, a lot of the pits of stone fruits contain a massive amount of cyanide, and if someone ingests enough of them, they can die?"

"Stone fruits?" I asked. "Like what?"

"Cherries, apricots, peaches ..."

"No, but they're hard. I just about broke my tooth on a cherry pit."

"Not if they're ground up."

I thought about that for a moment. "Are you saying someone ground up some cherry or peach pits and fed them to the passengers?"

"Not exactly, but the authorities doing the investigation have discovered that the passengers who died had consumed a large amount of cyanide, and they're not able to find any source that might have sold it to them. So now they're wondering if the murderer got it from a more natural source. It would still take quite a bit of it to kill someone."

"So all the person would have to do is grind up a cherry pit and add it to someone's food or drink?"

"It would take more than one."

"That just sounds weird to me."

"I know, right?" Summer paused. "Sorry I hijacked

the conversation, but I couldn't wait to tell you what I'd learned. So what's up?"

I told her about Andrea's odd behavior and how she'd gone through my luggage."

"Is anything missing?"

"Not as far as I can tell. Looked to me like she was hunting for something specific."

"I wonder what that could be."

"Well, there is something else I learned," Summer said. "Ever since the ship went back into commission, there's been law enforcement onboard."

"Isn't there always?"

"I think the cruise lines hire security, but I'm talking investigators who are planted to find clues and step in when needed."

"Oh." I thought about all the people I'd encountered, and I couldn't recall anyone who looked the slightest bit like an investigator. "I haven't seen anyone who—"

"Who looks like an investigator?" Summer chuckled. "I remember people saying I didn't look like a detective, which was why I was so good at going undercover."

"Good point. I wonder who it is."

"Are there any passengers who stand back and watch everyone else?"

"I can't think of anyone."

"Have you noticed that the same people are always present when the turmoil increases?"

I had to think for a moment before answering. "Yes, in fact, insanity seems to follow Betty."

"Maybe it's Betty."

She seemed to be the least likely. "I don't think it's her."

"Okay, so does anyone seem unduly interested in conversations that don't appear related to them?"

"Once again, Betty. But I can't imagine her in law enforcement."

"Maybe she's a plant," Summer said. "Remember they come in all shapes, sizes, and ages. Plus it's expensive to live on a ship full-time. Does she appear wealthy enough to throw her money away like that?"

"She doesn't appear terribly wealthy, but she said her sister is helping her out with the expenses."

"Her sister? Why would she do that?"

"Oh, sorry, I forgot to tell you that Betty's sister Myrna is married to the captain, and she showed up unexpectedly. Betty was shocked."

"What? Start over and tell me everything from the beginning."

I spent the next couple of minutes telling her about Myrna surprising everyone. She asked a few questions that I answered, until I couldn't think of anything else.

"You do realize, there's a lot of good stuff here. I would do anything to be there right now."

"You're incorrigible, Summer. I've never seen anyone but you get so excited about finding a murderer."

"I'm afraid it's in my blood." She laughed. "But I suppose that's better than having cyanide in my blood."

"So what should I do now?"

"Watch for signs of someone taking notes or using their cell phone more than normal. You also need to pay attention to someone who always comes to the rescue—especially if they appear out of the blue. And when someone suddenly takes extra time getting to know you or anyone else when there isn't any reason, they just might be fishing for facts related to the investigation."

"Wouldn't that be too obvious?" I asked.

"Only if you were suspicious. You'd be surprised by how few people realize they're being questioned by law enforcement."

I thought about Betty and how nosy she'd been. "So you think Betty might be in law enforcement?"

"Could be, but there's no way I can be sure unless I'm there."

"When can you be here?"

Again, Summer laughed. "You should have asked me before you went. But I can't just up and leave."

"I know. So what else do I need to do?"

"The most important thing is to pay attention to everyone and everything. Try to avoid being in a position of having people standing behind you."

"The old back-to-the-wall thing, huh?"

"Exactly." She paused for a few seconds. "One last thing I want to recommend is to be careful what you eat. Don't take anything from another passenger."

"I'm almost afraid to eat anything after what's been going on."

"I totally understand," Summer said. "I'd be the

same way."

"All these phone calls are going to cost me a fortune, so I'd better get off for now."

"If you need help with your phone bill, just holler."

After I disconnected the call, I smiled because I knew that Summer meant what she'd said—that she'd be willing to pay all or part of my phone bill. She'd always been that kind of person—helpful to a fault. She was one of those people who went into law enforcement because she truly wanted to make the world a better place. And I had no doubt that many lives had been touched and improved by her mere presence.

I was about to change into my pajamas when another knock came at my door. I froze in place for a few seconds before I decided to find out who it was.

Before I had a chance to say a word, I heard Betty hollering, "Autumn, you and I need to have a talk. Open up, will you? I know you're in there."

Chapter 23

I opened the door and let Betty in. Before I had a chance to close it, she grabbed it and slammed it shut.

"What's wrong?" I asked.

"I wish I knew. The captain came to my cabin and demanded more of my cherry brandy."

"More of it? Are you saying he drinks a lot of brandy?"

Betty shrugged. "I have no idea what he's doing with it, but I sure have given him a lot of bottles of it lately."

Something about that comment stuck in my head, and I had the feeling there was something about it that could possibly help me figure out what's going on. "Did you give it to him?"

"No. I'm almost out of it. I have one small bottle left, and I like to keep at least a little for myself ..." She gave me a sheepish look. "For medicinal purposes, of course."

"Yes, of course. When and where do you make it?"

"Between some of the cruises, I go to my house to make sure everything is taken care of. That's when I go on a brandy-making spree. You should see the bottles all lined up on the table and counters." She grinned. "So pretty."

"All cherry brandy?"

She nodded. "That's the only kind I know how to make."

"I'm sure you do a good job with it."

"Yes, I most certainly do. But there's something else I wanted to tell you about the captain."

"What's that?"

Betty squeezed her eyes shut as she closed her eyes momentarily. "He told me he understood when I said I only had one bottle left, but he wanted to see the bottle I was keeping. At first, I told him no, but he said he just wanted to see if it was as weak as what I was giving everyone else. I told him I didn't make weak brandy, and he said he didn't believe me. So I got the bottle and showed it to him." She shook her head.

"What happened then?"

"He yanked it out of my hand and took it into the bathroom. I had no idea what was going on, but he came back out and gave me back the full bottle. He even apologized for acting so rude, saying he wasn't himself lately after Myrna surprised him."

"Did he drink any of it?"

"If he did, I don't think he drank much."

I kept thinking about what Summer had told me, that cherry pits contained cyanide. As I thought about the possibility that we might have just stumbled on a big clue, I experienced that increasingly familiar feeling of goose bumps traveling up my arm.

"What's going on, Autumn?" Betty narrowed her eyes as she yanked me around to face her. "You look like you're about to be sick … or you're up to something."

"What all do you put in your cherry brandy?"

"I'm sorry, Autumn, but I can't tell you. It's a family secret."

I let out a sigh of frustration. "Seriously, Betty, just tell me one thing. Do you ever add the cherry pits?"

She gave a half shrug. "Maybe just a little."

"How do you process the pit?"

"I put it in my coffee grinder and pulverize it until it's a fine powder."

"Why do you add the pit?"

"Aren't you the curious one?" She chuckled. "I suppose that must be the teacher in you. At any rate, my late husband liked a little bit of the pit in there. He said it gave it a richer, nuttier flavor."

"Like how much is a little bit?"

She chewed on the inside of her cheek momentarily as she pondered it. "Like maybe one pit per bottle."

"How many drinks can you get from one bottle?"

Her face scrunched up as she thought about it. "All depends on how much someone drinks, but the average person would probably get at least ten or twelve."

I remembered Summer saying it would take a lot more than one pit to kill someone. "Are you sure there's only one pit in each bottle?"

"Positive. In fact, I don't even think there's that much in there." Betty tilted her head. "I understand that you enjoy learning new things, but why are you asking about cherry pits?"

I didn't think Betty was trying to kill anyone, but I still wasn't sure, so I didn't tell her. "Just curious."

A slow grin spread across her lips. "You want me to tell you my secret recipe, don't you?"

"Something like that." The last thing I wanted at the moment was her brandy recipe, but I needed to figure out if there was any chance Betty's cherry brandy had played a part in people getting so sick.

"How much do you charge for the brandy?" I asked.

"Charge?" She gave me an incredulous look. "What makes you think I charge for it? I don't ask anyone for a dime."

"You just give it to them?"

She nodded. "I like to make people happy, and my cherry brandy seems to do just that."

"I wonder why the captain is demanding more brandy," I said.

"That's what I'd like to know. He hasn't seemed intoxicated, so I assume he's giving it to others." She frowned. "I just hope he tells people where it came from and doesn't take all the credit for himself."

I was thinking the opposite. There might have been a time when I suspected Betty was guilty, but now my thoughts had changed. In fact, I would have been shocked if she was the one trying to poison people.

Betty walked over to the door, opened it a couple of inches, and glanced toward her cabin. She looked over her shoulder at me and gave me a thumbs-up gesture. "Looks like the coast is clear. I think I'll go on back to my cabin now. I hope I didn't upset you too much, Autumn." She started to go before stopping and turning back to face me. "I wish I had some brandy to leave with you. Maybe next time ..." Her voice trailed off as she left my cabin.

I stood in one spot staring at the door for several seconds before I made the decision to call Summer one more time. As I told her what all Betty had said, she gave me some instructions on what to do. I jotted everything down and stuck the paper in my pocket.

"Be alert at all times," she said. "We might have narrowed down the suspect list, but I've seen some surprises during my career. I don't want you to get hurt."

"Trust me, Summer. I'll be extremely careful."

After we hung up, I rubbed the back of my neck as I thought about how expensive my next cell phone bill would be. Then I pulled out the list and glanced at it to figure out what to do first.

Summer had told me to maintain a connection with Andrea. She didn't think Andrea was guilty—and neither did I—but she was certain that she was involved in some manner.

*

The next morning, I went straight to the cruise director's office, hoping to find Andrea. A woman sitting at the desk smiled and shook her head. "You might find her in the dining room."

I thanked her before doing an about face to have some breakfast. As soon as I entered the dining room, I spotted Andrea talking to the purser. She was showing him something on her phone, and he had a look of intensity that I hadn't seen on him before. Now I had no idea what to do.

Summer's words rang in my head. She'd told me to stay connected with Andrea, so I lifted my chin, squared my shoulders, and walked straight toward her.

Jerome spotted me first. My heart pounded at the thought of him telling me to go away, but he didn't. Instead, he smiled and gestured for me to join them.

"So how are you feeling this morning?" he asked. "Better, I hope."

I nodded as I racked my brain to come up with something to say. "Yes, I'm doing better."

"Good." He smiled at Andrea. "Why don't the two of you have breakfast together? I have some business to attend to."

Andrea's eager nod seemed strange, but I was relieved I didn't have to ask and risk being rejected. She held out her hand toward the room. "Why don't we sit at your regular table?"

Once we were seated, she looked me in the eyes. "Why do I get the feeling there's something on your mind? Do you have something to tell me?"

My heart thudded in my chest. I had no idea how to answer her.

"Are you worried about something?"

I started to shake my head, but the intensity of her stare did something to me. "I'm not sure."

"Well, I know you wanted to go back home—" The sound of someone hollering at the entrance interrupted her. She jumped up. "Sorry, Autumn. Gotta run."

Chapter 24

When I realized Jerome was the one who hollered, I jumped up and ran after them. They led me straight to the infirmary, where Doc Healey stood over another woman sprawled out on the floor. As I got closer, I realized it was Betty. My blood ran cold.

"Has anyone seen the captain?" Andrea asked.

"Nope." Doc Healey shook his head as he and Jerome lifted Betty onto a gurney. It took him a couple of minutes to get an IV in her arm.

As I watched, my mind raced back to what Betty had said—that the captain had come to her cabin and taken her last bottle of cherry brandy into the bathroom. Now, there was no doubt in my mind that he was the guilty one, but I had no idea who to tell.

Doc glanced at me, and his eyes widened. "Looks like Autumn is about to pass out. Andrea, get her a chair and get her some water."

I shook my head. "No, I'm fine. I just ... I think I know—" I stopped and clamped my mouth shut when I heard Betty moan.

"She's coming to," Doc Healey said as he leaned over Betty. "Can you hear me?"

"I hear you. What happened?" She coughed and moaned again. "My stomach."

I hopped up and went over to her. "Did you drink some of that brandy you were saving?"

She nodded as the doctor tried to push me away. "Can't you see she's not up to talking?"

Andrea joined us. "This is important, Charlie. Let Autumn talk to her."

"But—"

It took several minutes, but Betty finally managed to say that she'd consumed half of the last bottle of brandy after she went back to her cabin. I turned to face Andrea. "We need to find the captain."

Andrea touched my arm. "Why?"

"Because he's the one who is trying to kill people." Those words came out of my mouth before I had a chance to talk, and there was no taking them back now.

"What makes you think it was the captain?" Jerome asked, his voice deeper and more commanding than I remembered.

It took me a few minutes to explain what had happened. I told them what Summer had told me about the cherry pits.

Andrea and Jerome both turned to Doc Healey, who nodded. "It's possible. It would take an awful lot of cherry pits to kill someone unless they had a weakened immune system, but it can happen."

Andrea didn't bother trying to hide her phone as she looked at me with a completely different expression. It was stronger, more calculated, and one I'd seen on Summer more than once. I tilted my head and took a long, hard look at her.

"Who are you?" I asked.

She glanced at Jerome who nodded. The purser pulled something out of his pocket, and Andrea followed, reaching into her purse. They both flashed badges, letting me know they were law enforcement.

"But how—?" I looked back and forth between them several times.

"We've been undercover ever since those people died several months ago," Andrea said in a professional tone.

"But I thought there was a supergerm."

Andrea smiled. "That's what we wanted people to think." She exchanged a look with Jerome. "Looks like it worked."

"Is Doc Healey also undercover?" I asked

The doctor flashed a brief smile. "Not in this lifetime. I'm a real doctor."

"Did you know about Andrea and Jerome?" I asked.

He flashed each of them an apologetic look before facing me. "I had my suspicions."

Jerome held up a finger as he headed toward the door. "I'll be back in a few."

I looked at Andrea. "Where's he going?"

She gave me a warm smile. "The helicopter is about to land, and then they're going to find the captain." She leaned closer to me. "Are you okay? Do you want me to get something for you?"

"No thanks. I'm fine."

"By the way, I left the pitcher of water in your room—the one you had the security guy check for fingerprints."

"But why?" I asked.

She shrugged. "I figured you might be thirsty after all that hyperventilating you've been doing."

I laughed. "I do tend to breathe more through my mouth when I'm nervous or excited."

"A lot of people do." Andrea paused. "Do you realize that you just might have solved a crime that has baffled hundreds of trained professionals? We suspected it had something to do with the brandy, but our tests didn't show a dangerous amount of cyanide in any of the bottles we analyzed." Andrea shook her head. "Are you sure you're a teacher and not a detective?"

I told her all about my cousin. "And I have to admit she's talked me through this, or I never would have figured it out on my own."

"She might have told you about the cherry pits having cyanide, but you put it all together."

I didn't like taking credit for something so big, but who was I to argue? "I'm just glad we know what's going on."

The shadow of someone at the door caught our attention. I glanced up and spotted Myrna. "Where's my sister? I heard she almost died."

"On the gurney." I gestured toward Betty, so she

walked right up to her.

"Be gentle," Doc Healey said.

The look on Myrna's face was quite different from what I'd seen in the past. Instead of the animosity she'd shown last time she was with her sister, I saw grave concern. "My sweet baby sister. I freaked out when I heard you were here."

Betty's colorless lips broke into a half smile. "It's about time you freaked out." She moaned again. "Too bad I have to be at death's door to get your attention."

Everyone's attention snapped back to Myrna. I held my breath until she spoke. "You've always had my attention." She reached for Betty's hand and squeezed it. "And I think you know I love you."

Betty lifted her head and looked around the room until she spotted me. She winked before looking back at her sister. "You do realize I have witnesses of you saying that."

At that moment, Jerome burst back into the room. "We found the captain, and he's in custody."

"What?" Myrna straightened up and shoved her fist onto her hip. "Why would my husband be in custody? What on earth did he do?"

Andrea pursed her lips as she cast a brief glance at me before approaching Myrna. "Come on. Let's go to my office, and I'll tell you all about it." They got to the door before Andrea glanced over her shoulder at me. "By the way, I'm the one who was in your cabin."

"What were you doing in my cabin?"

She grimaced. "I was looking for a bottle of brandy. We knew you'd made friends with Betty, so we thought you might have some, and we already had an idea that the brandy had something to do with the investigation."

"I tried to give her some, but she wouldn't take it." Betty stopped talking and let out another moan. "Smart girl."

Epilogue

"Wow!" Summer smiled as she looked at me in amazement. "What an exciting vacation. You couldn't have planned that if you tried."

"Exciting, yes." I sighed. "Relaxing, no. Now I need a vacation to recover."

"How about another cruise?" she asked, giving me a sly look.

I held out both of my hands, palms facing her. "No way. Never again."

Summer chuckled. "Never say never."

I'd only been back home for a day, but Summer couldn't stay away. She had to find out all the nitty gritty details. I told her everything about all the different people I'd met.

"Interesting how so many murders are motivated by passion or greed," Summer said. "Or both."

"I know." I grimaced. "I remembered you saying that several times through the years. That's one of the reasons I thought it might have been someone else."

"It *was* motivated by passion," Summer reminded me.

"Well, yeah, I suppose it was, indirectly. The captain was worried about his wife finding out about his passion."

Summer nodded. "Fear of passion discovery. The captain clearly wanted to avoid his wife finding out about his trysts."

"I'm surprised by how many women would have anything to do with him romantically. He's not terribly good looking or even very nice."

"But he has power."

"Power?" I gave her a curious look. "How do you figure that?"

"He's in charge of the ship. That's a lot of power when you're out at sea."

"Yeah, that's true, but still ..." I shuddered at the memory of how he'd asked me to have dinner at the Captain's Table.

Summer paced a couple of times before stopping and looking me in the eyes. "You do realize that if the captain had stopped sooner, he might never have gotten caught."

"How do you figure?"

"It wasn't until this last cruise that the authorities managed to get a bottle with the cherry pits he ground up and added."

"I wonder if it tasted any different."

She lifted an eyebrow and gave me a goofy look. "Wanna taste it and let me know?"

"No way."

"But there is one thing that has me baffled." Summer tapped her chin. "So why was Aileen's lipstick in Harvey's pocket?"

"Well ..." I paused until she glared at me, and then I laughed. "Harvey said the captain had given it to him to hold for a while, but I'm not so sure I believe him."

"Was Aileen that big of a vamp?" Summer asked.

Again, I laughed. "She'd like to think she is."

A look of amusement flashed across her face. "Next time you go somewhere, I want to go."

"I thought you were thinking about going back to the police department."

She shrugged. "That's a big decision that I can't take lightly. If I change my mind and leave again, that'll be the end of any chance of my having a law enforcement career."

"Yeah, as if that'll ever happen. Even if it's not official, you'll always be a detective."

"Don't forget who actually solved this last crime." She pursed her lips and made a silly face. "Now you've crossed over to my side ... and you've become quite a detective yourself."

"No!" I feigned horror. "Say it isn't so."

"Afraid it is, cuz." She laughed as she gave me a hug. "Gotta run. Give me a call if you run across any more bodies."

After Summer left my apartment, I sank down in my favorite chair. I was exhausted beyond belief after such a frightening ordeal, but I had to admit, there was something exhilarating about being involved in solving a crime.

The End

Printed in Great Britain
by Amazon